DAVID GOLDER

Irène Némirovsky was born in Kiev in 1903, the daughter of a successful Jewish banker. In 1918 her family fled the Russian Revolution for France where she became a bestselling novelist. Prevented from publishing when the Germans occupied France in 1940, she moved with her husband and two small daughters from Paris to the safety of the small village of Issy-l'Evêque (in German occupied territory). It was here that Irène began writing *Suite Française*, published to wide acclaim in 2005. She died in Auschwitz in 1942.

ALSO BY IRÈNE NÉMIROVSKY

Suite Française

IRÈNE NÉMIROVSKY

David Golder

Translated from the French by Sandra Smith

With an Introduction by Patrick Marnham

VINTAGE BOOKS

London

Published by Vintage 2007

2 4 6 8 10 9 7 5 3 1

Copyright © Éditions Bernard Grasset, 1929
Translation copyright © Sandra Smith, 2007
Introduction © Patrick Marnham, 2007

License arranged by the French Publishers' Agency in New York

First published in France by Éditions Bernard Grasset in 1929

First published in Great Britain in 2007 by Vintage

Vintage
Random House, 20 Vauxhall Bridge Road,
London SW1V 2SA

www.randomhouse.co.uk

Addresses for companies within
The Random House Group Limited can be found at:
www.randomhouse.co.uk/offices.htm

The Random House Group Limited Reg. No. 954009

A CIP catalogue record for this book
is available from the British Library

ISBN 9780099493969

The Random House Group Limited makes every effort to ensure
that the papers used in its books are made from trees that have been
legally sourced from well-managed and credibly certified forests.
Our paper procurement policy can be found at:
www.randomhouse.co.uk/paper.htm

Typeset by Palimpsest Book Production Limited,
Grangemouth, Stirlingshire

Printed and bound in Great Britain by
Bookmarque Ltd, Croydon, Surrey

Introduction

Irène Némirovsky died in Auschwitz in 1942. Despite her status in the 1930s as one of France's most popular novelists, her name had been largely forgotten until the recent discovery and posthumous publication of her unfinished masterpiece *Suite Française*. This fictional account of the fall of France in 1940 and the first years of the wartime German Occupation was published in Paris in 2004 to national acclaim, and subsequently became a worldwide bestseller. It has led to a new interest in the work of Némirovsky, a Russian émigré whose family had moved to France after the Revolution of 1917.

Irène Némirovsky had published thirteen successful novels in France before the Nazis introduced their wartime ban on Jewish authors, but it was with the second, *David Golder* (1929), that she really made her mark. Completed when she was only twenty-six, it was accepted by the leading house of Grasset and greatly impressed critics with its maturity. The central character was compared to Balzac's Père Goriot, the book was turned into a play and a film (starring Harry Baur), and an English translation appeared in Britain and America in 1930. The *New York Times* hailed Némirovsky as a successor to Dostoyevsky. Her career prospered and before long she was earning two or three times as much as her husband, who was a banker.

David Golder is the story of a powerful financier – brutal, solitary and ruthless – who has risen from poverty in Russia to a controlling position in the international oil business by sacrificing everything to the pursuit of wealth. Such brooding and malevolent figures recur in nineteenth- and twentieth-century literature; they were portrayed by Zola and Trollope, and later by Graham Greene, among others. For these writers, the world of high finance threatened, conspired and devoured, and the character of David Golder is one of its most effective representatives. In Némirovsky's case, the portrait is the more convincing because it is executed from the inside, for this was to some extent her world.

Irène Némirovsky was born in Kiev in 1903. Her father, Léon – who was a self-made banker – was among the few Jews who were *persona grata* at the Imperial Court of St Petersburg. Irène was brought up speaking fluent French. With the outbreak of the Bolshevik Revolution in 1917, Léon Némirovsky was proscribed and the family had to go into hiding. They lost everything and fled disguised as peasants, first to Finland and Sweden, then to France – which they reached by sea after nearly losing their lives in a violent storm. In Paris, Léon managed to rebuild their fortunes by taking a job as manager in a branch of the bank he had once owned. Among other interests, Léon's bank – like Golder's finance house – speculated in oil fields. Irène would have witnessed at first hand the kind of ruthlessness necessary to survive in the business world. Furthermore, it is clear from Némirovsky's other fiction that she had seen for herself the wretched environment into which Golder was born. Kiev under the Tsars was a city of pogroms, and the Némirovsky's plight during the Revolution gave the fourteen-year-old Irène a taste of the same fear. It was this experience that enabled her to draw such a vivid picture of the extremes to which men like Golder could be driven in order to escape their roots.

In the opening chapter of the novel, Golder refuses to take pity on Marcus, his partner of twenty-six years. Their meeting is apparently devoted to the lifeless details of a financial negotiation. Almost immediately Némirovsky reveals that the former partners are in fact engaged in a pitiless struggle for survival. 'I needed the money David [. . .] I . . . I'm really desperate for money,' Marcus explains, but Golder's answer remains 'No', the opening word of the book. There is pathos in Marcus's confession; money, blood, air, life, Marcus needs them as much as anyone else, and Golder, watching him suffocate, declines to help. Golder is the sort of man whose day is brightened when he sees a fellow human being in trouble. When Golder gets the better of a weaker opponent, he is dangerous. 'If you only knew how many he has ruined, driven to suicide or condemned to misery,' Gloria – Golder's wife – objects when her lover refers to Golder as 'a good man'.

Némirovsky describes Golder as 'an enormous man in his late sixties'. He has 'flabby arms and legs, piercing eyes the colour of water, thick white hair and a ravaged face so hard it looked as if it had been hewn from stone by a rough, clumsy hand.' As a young man, Golder had been a thin little Jew with red hair and pale eyes, holes in his shoes and empty pockets, hawking rags and scrap from a sack on his back. In the struggle for survival his senses have become fine-tuned to the presence or absence of money, he can sniff it out: '"He must be rolling in it again, the pig," thought Golder. (He knew how to recognise the inimitable, telling little tremor in a man's voice that gives away his emotion even if his words appear indifferent.)' Golder now lives in what seems to be an enviable world, a world of large apartments, spacious villas, sumptuous women and fast cars, where he is feared and obeyed. But it is an empty place. In this society of rootless exiles, money transcends all personal values and becomes the measure of everything – love, strength and self-esteem. The women in Golder's world are from the same mould. Idle and pampered, they are just as greedy as their husbands but less energetic. Golder's daughter, Joyce, is the only person he cares for, but even she avoids his company unless she is short of funds. There are two lyrical interludes in the story. Both take place in a garden on a hot night; both involve intimacy between a man and a woman who trust each other enough to drop their guard; neither involves David Golder. The only intimacy he shares with his wife Gloria is the intimacy of murderous anger.

And yet the monster is human, a fact that emerges slowly as Némirovsky shows us Golder's black humour and his vulnerability. The humour starts with the preparations for the funeral of Golder's victim Marcus which, seen through Golder's eyes, are neither tragic nor pathetic, but almost hilarious. When Golder arrives to pay his last respects he finds that the widow is with the corpse; waiting nearby, he thinks he can hear the murmur of prayers, then realises that it is not the rabbi but the undertaker: Marcus's widow is objecting to the price of the coffin. There is a smell in the house that Golder does not recognise and he is uneasy – unsure whether it comes from the flowers or the corpse. Eventually, and with the greatest reluctance, he meets the widow, but instead of reproaching Golder for his inhumanity, she reveals that Marcus caused major inconvenience by shooting himself in a notorious brothel – 'as if going bankrupt weren't enough'. Golder remains unmoved. ' "She must be very rich," thought Golder, "the old crow. [. . .] He pictured his own wife quickly hiding her chequebook whenever he came into the room, as if it were a packet of love letters.' Golder is no respecter of persons, he is too observant to be duped; invited by Joyce to meet her new flame, Prince Alexis, who expects to be addressed as 'Your Imperial Highness', Golder takes one look at the youth and grunts, 'Where did that little gigolo come from?'

The humour is further emphasised in the character of Golder's friend Soifer, an 'old German Jew' who made a fortune, lost it and won it back, and who will die alone and be buried without a wreath by the family he hates and which hates him in its turn but to which he has nonetheless left all his money – thus fulfilling 'the incomprehensible destiny of every good Jew on this earth'. Soifer, unlike Golder, is a type; we see him in silhouette, without any insight. He walks on tiptoe to save on shoe leather and complains that his wife has bought a new hat that looks like an upturned flowerpot when, at her age, she would have been better advised to buy a shroud. If Golder's doorbell rings in the middle of the night, he assumes that Soifer, having suffered an accident, has refused to pay the doctor so that he, Golder, is being dunned for the bill. Soifer grows indignant because the French police have told him to renew his identity card or face expulsion. Where would I go at my age, he asks. 'To Germany,' Golder suggests. 'Germany can go to hell!' Soifer replies. 'You know what happened to me before in Germany, when I had that trouble over providing them with war supplies.' Soifer invites Golder to join him in a kosher restaurant where they serve the best stuffed pike in Paris, and Golder tells him he's not eating meat or fish. 'No one's asking you to eat anything,' says the wealthy miser, 'just come and pay.' 'Go to hell,' says Golder. But they turn into the Rue des Rosiers, in the Jewish quarter, and breathe the odour of poverty – dust, fish and rotten straw. 'A dirty Jewish neighbourhood, isn't it?' says Soifer, affectionately. 'Does it remind you of anything?' 'Nothing good,' replies Golder, and later he sighs, 'It's a long road.' 'Yes,' agrees the millionaire Soifer, 'long, hard and pointless . . .' This is the world of Jewish exiles in 1920s Paris – unsentimental, bitter and black.

But it was not a Jewish world with which Némirovsky identified. As she began to gain confidence in France – and her family recovered some of its wealth – Jewishness became, in some ways, as distant to her as it was to her bourgeois Catholic neighbours in the fashionable quarters of Paris and

Biarritz. In 1926 she married Michael Epstein, also an exile and also of Russian Jewish banking stock, but although they chose a religious ceremony in a Paris synagogue, their children were not brought up in the Jewish faith. When Némirovsky arrived in Paris in 1919, she had two goals. The first was to establish herself as a French writer. The second was assimilation, the norm of that time for Jewish people of her class and education. In the aftermath of the Dreyfus Affair, when a French army officer was falsely accused and convicted of treason because he was Jewish, the defensive reflex of the French Jewish community was not to proclaim its difference; it was to insist that Jews were just as French as anyone else. 'L'Affaire', as the Dreyfus case was known, divided French society into those who were against Dreyfus and who instinctively defended military honour, and those (often members of the same family) who defended Dreyfus and attacked injustice. After a bitter twelve-year struggle, Dreyfus was acquitted and rehabilitated, and the process of Jewish assimilation could continue. This process was common across Europe. In Austria-Hungary, the novelist Joseph Roth believed that Jews could escape marginalisation by appealing to the protection of their sovereign, the Emperor, some going so far as to convert to Catholicism or Lutheran deism. In Germany, the family of the historian Fritz Stern converted to Lutheran Christianity; the Sterns worshipped on Sundays as did the Reform Jews, and the two congregations – Christian and Reform Jewish – said similar prayers and celebrated religious festivals such as Christmas and Hanukah together before decorated trees. The model of assimilation was the natural choice for the Némirovskys, who regarded it as a routine that had been interrupted by the Bolshevik Revolution. Irène Némirovsky had loved France since childhood; now she wanted to become entirely French, and her father's wealth and *savoir-faire* gave her the freedom to make that choice. If it entailed a partial repudiation of her public identity, she was prepared to do that, although her private sense of who she was remained unchanged.

In choosing to write a novel in which the central character, David Golder, was a hated Jewish financier, Irène Némirovsky was playing with fire. By 1929, the year of publication, she had lived in France quite long enough to know that anti-Semitism was still a powerful force in French politics and that it was entrenched in monarchist, patriotic and Catholic opinion. The Great War of 1914–18 had done something to heal the wounds left by the Dreyfus Affair; the French nation at war had been bound in *l'Union sacrée*, Jew and Christian, Catholic and republican, all against *les Boches*. 'L'Action Française', the newspaper of the monarchist and nationalist movement, which could normally be relied on to stand by its anti-Semitism, went out of its way after the War to praise the Jewish heroes who had fought for France. Hatred of the invader seemed for a time to have exhausted the national supply of fear and loathing. This new spirit of tolerance was put to the test when heavy post-War immigration coincided with a period of steeply rising unemployment. 720,000 Italians, mostly communists or anti-fascist activists, had settled in southern France by 1936, without attracting any criticism from the French right. But when, during the same period, Jewish immigration from Poland and Eastern Europe increased the size of the native community by about 100,000, the figures were wildly exaggerated in the anti-Semitic press. The popular success of *David Golder* delighted some French anti-Semites and alarmed some Jewish critics, concerned about stereotyping. The latter may well have felt justified in their alarm when the Stavisky affair provoked a political crisis in 1933. Serge Stavisky could have stepped straight out of the pages of *David Golder*. He was a real-life Jewish swindler who had been born in Kiev then taken French citizenship before setting out to make his fortune by issuing false bonds and bribing judges and politicians. When he was exposed, he committed suicide, having stolen over 250 million francs and ruined thousands of small investors. In the ensuing riots of February 1934, fifteen people were killed in the streets of Paris, and the scandal caused the downfall of two successive Radical governments.

Later, Irène Némirovsky said that she would not have written *David Golder* in the same way after Hitler's rise to power. But she remained a high-spirited young woman, confident in her own judgement and determined to continue writing about what she knew. In pre-Second World War France, she was surrounded by anti-Semitism; it was in the air, and she responded by adopting its conventions and then breaking through the crust of prejudice to discover the real people imprisoned beneath. Golder is Jewish because Némirovsky was Jewish, but her choice of an unsympathetic Jewish character did not make Némirovsky anti-Semitic any more than Robert Louis Stevenson was anti-Scottish because he created the diabolical figure of Ebenezer in *Kidnapped*. Men like Golder existed, and no doubt still exist. They had come a very long way, just how long we discover in the novel's devastating climax. They had done it by themselves, trusting no one. Golder was a risk taker who lived by bluff and who could not afford to show any weakness. When he does reveal what he truly cares about, he gives his most dangerous enemy her chance, and he pays a heavy price. In showing us the vulnerability behind Golder's mask, the humanity of a powerful Jewish villain, Némirovsky was rewriting *The Merchant of Venice*, but in her version Portia speaks for Shylock. By undermining the assumptions of the anti-Semitic right, Némirovsky was playing a skilful double game that would have done nothing to decrease her sales, just as the manner of Golder's ultimate redemption would have done nothing to strengthen her readers' anti-Semitism.

Throughout the 1930s, Némirovsky followed French

politics with an informed Parisian eye, using the decadence and corruption of the Third Republic as a theme for her later fiction. But she continued to trust in assimilation and in the protection offered by the French nation, believing that she was safe in the country she loved – a country that had served as her family's refuge, and had rewarded her talent with wealth and fame. The first sign of uneasiness came after the Munich Crisis of 1938. The two daughters of Némirovsky's marriage to Michael Epstein were French by birth. Now, as rumours of war grew louder, Irène and her husband applied for French citizenship. Their application, though well-supported, received no response and so in 1939 – in a final commitment to assimilation – Irène and her children converted to Catholicism.

Before he was shot by a German firing squad in 1944, the historian and resister Marc Bloch wrote in his will, 'Faced with death I declare that I was born Jewish, that it has never occurred to me to deny it ... but that throughout my life I have felt myself to be above all and quite simply a Frenchman.' This was the same identity claimed by Irène Némirovsky, and today the novel *David Golder* – seventy-seven years after it was first published – has become an historical document and a testament to the tragic error that led directly to its author's death. Némirovsky never denied her Jewish origins. After the fall of France, she watched as her chosen refuge turned into a death trap. The Vichy regime passed a succession of anti-Semitic laws. Her husband lost his job. Her own novels were banned. She and her family left Paris for the supposed safety of the countryside, where they were all forced to wear the Yellow Star. And then the German authorities and the French government signed a joint agreement to round up and deport foreign Jews. During this period Némirovsky started working on *Suite Française* and wrote in her notebook, 'Since [this country] rejects me let us watch it lose its honour and its life.' But she also felt sorry for the German soldiers leaving her village for the Russian Front, and wrote, 'I am resolved never again to hold rancour, however justified, towards a group of people, whatever their race, religion, convictions, prejudices or errors.'

Irène Némirovsky was arrested by French police on 13 July, 1942 and deported from France within four days of her arrest. One month later she was dead. Her husband, knowing nothing of her fate, struggled desperately to find her, believing that her arrest must have been a mistake. But the only error had been her own, the error of a misplaced trust in civilised standards and humanity, the same sense of humanity that Irène Némirovsky so skilfully deployed in defence of the central character in this book.

Patrick Marnham, December 2006

* For information about the life of Irène Némirovsky, I am grateful for the assistance of her daughter Madame Denise Epstein; to Olivier Philipponnat and Patrick Lienhardt, authors of a forthcoming biography, and to their publisher, Éditions Grasset. Other biographical sources include the preface to *Suite Française* (Éditions Denoel) by Myriam Anissimov and *Irène Némirovsky: Her Life and Works* by Jonathan Weiss (Stanford University Press, 2006).

'No,' said Golder, tilting his desklamp so that the light shone directly into the face of Simon Marcus who was sitting opposite him on the other side of the table. For a moment Golder observed the wrinkles and lines that furrowed Marcus's swarthy face whenever he moved his lips or closed his eyes, like the ripples on dark water when the wind blows across it. But his hooded eyes with their Oriental langour remained calm, bored and indifferent. A face as unyielding as a wall. Golder carefully lowered the lamp's flexible metal stem.

'A hundred, Golder? Think about it. It's a good price,' said Marcus.

'No,' Golder murmured again, then added, 'I don't want to sell.'

Marcus laughed. His long white teeth, capped in gold, gleamed eerily in the darkness.

'How much were your famous oil shares worth in 1920 when you first bought them?' he drawled; his voice was nasal, sarcastic.

'I bought them at four hundred. And if those Soviet pigs had given the nationalised land back to the oil companies, I would have made a lot of money. Lang and his group were backing me. In 1913, the daily output from the Teisk region was already ten thousand tons . . . seriously. After the Genoa Conference, I remember my shares fell from four hundred

1

to one hundred and two ... After that ...' Golder made a vague gesture of frustration. 'But I held on to them ... Money was no object, in those days.'

'Yes, but now, in 1926, don't you realise that your Russian oil fields aren't worth shit to you? Well? I mean, it's not as if you have either the means or the inclination to go and run them yourself, is it? All you can hope to do is shift them for a higher price on the Stock Market ... A hundred is a good sum.'

Golder slowly rubbed his eyes; the smoke that filled the room had irritated them.

'No, I don't want to sell.' He spoke more quietly this time. 'I'll sell after Tübingen Petroleum signs the agreement for the concession in Teisk. I think you know the one I'm talking about ...'

Marcus mumbled what sounded like 'Ah, yes ...' and fell silent.

'You've been negotiating that deal behind my back since last year, Marcus,' Golder said slowly. 'You know you have ... I bet they offered you a good price for my shares once they closed the deal, didn't they?'

He said no more, for his heart was beating almost painfully, just as it did whenever he was winning. Marcus slowly stubbed out his cigar in the overflowing ashtray.

'If he suggests we go fifty-fifty,' Golder thought suddenly, 'it will all be over for him.'

He leaned forward so he could hear what Marcus was about to say. There was a brief silence, then Marcus spoke.

'Why don't we go halves, Golder?'

Golder clenched his teeth. 'Are you serious?'

'You know Golder, you shouldn't make another enemy,' Marcus murmured, lowering his eyes, 'You've got enough already.'

His hands were clutching the wooden table, and as they moved, his nails made short, sharp little scratching noises.

Beneath the light of the lamp, his long fingers with their heavy rings shone against the mahogany of the Empire desk; they were trembling.

Golder smiled. 'You're no longer very threatening, my friend . . .'

Marcus remained silent for a moment, carefully examining his manicured nails.

'Fifty-fifty David! What do you say? We've been partners for twenty-six years. Let's wipe the slate clean and start again. If you'd been here in December when Tübingen spoke to me . . .'

Golder fiddled with the telephone wire, winding it around his wrists.

'In December,' he repeated, frowning. 'How good of you . . . only . . .'

He said no more. Marcus knew as well as he did that in December he had been in America looking for investors in Golmar, the company that had bound them together for so many years, like a ball and chain.

'David, there's still time . . .' Marcus continued. 'Let's negotiate with the Soviets together, what do you say? It's a difficult business. We'll split everything down the middle – commissions, profits . . . How about it? That's fair, isn't it? David? Otherwise . . .'

He waited for some reply, an agreement, even an insult, but Golder's breathing was laboured and he said nothing.

'Listen,' Marcus whispered, 'Tübingen's not the only company in the world . . .' He touched Golder's unmoving arm as if to wake him. 'There are other companies, newer ones, and . . .' he searched for the right words. 'There are companies more willing to speculate, companies that didn't sign the 1922 Oil Agreement and who don't give a damn about who holds the old stock, you, for example . . . They could . . .'

'You mean Amrum Oil?' said Golder.

3

'Oh!' Marcus winced. 'So you know about that as well? Well, listen my friend, I'm sorry, but the Russians are going to sign with Amrum. Since you're now refusing to play ball, you can keep your shares in Teisk till Judgement Day. You can take them with you to your grave . . .'

'The Russians aren't going to sign with Amrum.'

'They've already signed,' cried Marcus.

Golder waved his hand. 'Yes, I know. A provisional agreement. But it was supposed to be ratified by Moscow within forty-five days. That was yesterday. Now it's all up in the air again, and you're worried, so you came to see what you could get out of me . . .' Golder started to cough. 'Let me explain it all to you. Tübingen right? He wasn't too happy when Amrum whipped those Persian oil fields out from under his feet two years ago. So, this time, I suspect he'd rather die than lose the fight. Actually, it hasn't been that difficult so far: just a question of offering a bit more to that little Jew who has been helping you negotiate with the Soviets. Give them a call right now, if you don't believe me . . .'

'You're lying, you pig!' shouted Marcus in the strange, shrill voice of an hysterical woman.

'Give them a call. You'll see.'

'And . . . what about Tübingen? Does the old man know?'

'Of course.'

'This is all your doing, you bastard, you crook!'

'Well, what did you expect? Think about it . . . Last year there was that oil deal in Mexico, and three years ago the high octane deal. How many millions went from my pocket into yours? And what did I say about it? Nothing. And then . . .' Golder seemed to be looking for more proof, attempting to bring everything together in his mind, but then he brushed it all aside with a shrug of the shoulders.

'Business,' was all he murmured, as if he were naming some terrifying god . . .

4

Marcus fell silent. He took a packet of cigarettes from the table, opened it and carefully struck a match. 'Why do you smoke these disgusting Gauloises, Golder, when you're as rich as you are?'

Golder watched Marcus's shaking hands as if he were contemplating the final death throes of a wounded animal.

'I needed the money David,' Marcus suddenly said in a different tone of voice, the corner of his mouth contorting into a grimace. 'I . . . I'm really desperate for money, David. Couldn't you . . . let me make just a little? Don't you think that . . .'

'No!'

Golder shook his fist in the air. He saw the pale hands clasp each other, the clenched fingers digging their nails into the flesh.

'You're ruining me,' Marcus said finally, in an odd, hollow voice.

Golder said nothing, refusing to look up. Marcus hesitated, then quietly pushed back his chair.

'Goodbye, David,' he said, and then shouted suddenly, 'What was that?'

'Nothing,' said Golder. 'Goodbye.'

Golder lit a cigarette, but put it out when he started choking on the first puff. His shoulders were wracked by a nervous, asthmatic cough, which filled his mouth with bitter phlegm. Blood rushed to his face, normally deathly pale and waxy, with dark circles under the eyes. Golder was an enormous man in his late sixties. He had flabby arms and legs, piercing eyes the colour of water, thick white hair and a ravaged face so hard it looked as if it had been hewn from stone by a rough, clumsy hand.

The room reeked of smoke and that smell of stale sweat that is particular to Parisian apartments in summer when they have been left empty for a long time.

Golder swivelled around in his chair and opened the window. For a long while, he looked out at the Eiffel Tower, all lit up. Its red glow streamed like blood down the cool dawn sky. He thought of Golmar. Six shimmering gold letters that tonight would be turning like suns in four of the world's greatest cities. Golmar: two names, his and Marcus's, merged together. He pursed his lips. 'Golmar . . . David Golder, alone, from now on . . .'

He reached for the notepad beside him and read the letterhead:

GOLDER & MARCUS
Buyers and Seller of Petroleum Products
Aviation Fuel. Unleaded, Leaded and Premium Gasoline
White-Spirit. Diesel. Lubricants.
New York, London, Paris, Berlin

Slowly he crossed out the first line and wrote 'David Golder', his heavy handwriting cutting into the paper. He was finally on his own. 'It's over, thank God,' he thought with relief. 'He'll go now . . .' Later on, after Teisk granted the concession to Tübingen, he would be part of the greatest oil company in the world, and then he would easily be able to rebuild Golmar.

Until then . . . He quickly scribbled down some figures. These past two years had been especially terrible. Lang's bankruptcy, the 1922 Agreement . . . At least he would no longer have to pay for Marcus's women, his jewellery, his debts . . . He had enough to pay for without him. How expensive this idiotic lifestyle was! His wife, his daughter, the houses in Biarritz and Paris . . . In Paris alone he was paying sixty thousand francs in rent, taxes. The furniture had cost more than a million when he'd bought it. For whom? No one lived there. Closed shutters, dust. He looked with a kind of hatred at certain objects he particularly detested: four lamps, Winged Victories in bronze with black marble bases; an enormous square inkstand, decorated with gilt bees – empty. It all had to be paid for, and where was he supposed to get the money?

'The fool,' he growled angrily. '"You're ruining me!" So what? I'm sixty-eight . . . Let *him* start over again. *I've* had to do it often enough . . .'

He turned his head sharply towards the large mirror above the cold fireplace, looking uneasily at his drawn features, at the mottled bluish patches on his pale skin, and the two folds sunk into the thick flesh around his mouth like the drooping jowls on an old dog. 'I'm getting old,' he grumbled bitterly, 'yes, I'm getting old. . .' For two or three years now he'd been getting tired more easily. 'I absolutely must get away tomorrow,' he thought. 'A week or ten days relaxing in Biarritz where I can be left in peace, otherwise I'm going to collapse.' He took his diary, propped it up on the table against a gold-framed photograph of a young girl and started leafing through it. It was full of names and dates, with 14 September underlined in ink. Tübingen was expecting him in London that day. That meant he could have barely a week in Biarritz . . . Then London, Moscow, London again, New York. He let out an irritated little moan, stared at his daughter's picture, sighed, then looked away and began rubbing his painful eyes, burning from weariness. He had got back from Berlin that day and for a long time now he hadn't been able to sleep on the train as he used to.

He stood up to head for the club, as always, but then realised it was after three o'clock in the morning. 'I'll just go to bed,' he thought. 'I'll be on the train again tomorrow . . .' He noticed a stack of letters that needed signing piled on the desk. He sat down again. Every evening he read over the letters his secretaries had prepared. They were a bunch of asses. But he preferred them that way. He thought of Marcus's secretary and smiled: Braun, a little Jew with fiery eyes, who had sold him the plans for the Amrum deal. He started to read, leaning very far forward under the lamp. His thick white hair used to be red, and a hint of that burning colour still remained at his temples and at the back of his neck, glowing, like a flame half-hidden beneath the ashes.

The telephone next to Golder's bed broke the silence with its long, shrill, interminable ringing, but Golder didn't wake up: in the mornings, he slept as deeply and heavily as a dead man. Finally he opened his eyes with a low groan and grabbed the receiver.

'Hello, hello . . .'

He carried on shouting 'Hello, hello', without recognising his secretary's voice, until he heard the words, 'Dead, Monsieur Golder . . . Monsieur Marcus is dead. . .'

He said nothing. 'Hello, can you hear me?' the voice continued. 'Monsieur Marcus is dead.'

'Dead,' Golder repeated slowly, while a strange little shiver ran down his spine. 'Dead . . . It isn't possible . . .'

'It happened last night, Monsieur . . . on the Rue Chabanais . . . Yes, in a brothel . . . He shot himself in the chest. They're saying that . . .'

Golder gently placed the receiver between the sheets and pressed the blanket over it, as if he wanted to smother the voice that he could still hear droning on like some enormous trapped fly.

Finally, there was silence.

Golder rang the bell. 'Run me a bath,' he said to the servant who came in with the post and breakfast tray, 'a cold bath.'

'Shall I pack your dinner jacket, Sir?'

Golder frowned nervously. 'Pack? Oh, yes, Biarritz . . . I

9

don't know. I may be going tomorrow, or perhaps the day after, I don't know . . .'

'I'll have to go to his house tomorrow,' he muttered. 'The funeral will be on Tuesday no doubt. Damn . . .' He swore quietly. The servant, in the adjoining room, was filling the bath. Golder swallowed a mouthful of hot tea, opened some letters at random, then threw the rest on the floor and stood up. He sat down in the bathroom, closed his dressing gown over his knees and absentmindedly twisted the tassels on his silk belt as he watched the flowing water with an engrossed, mournful look on his face.

'Dead . . . dead . . .'

Little by little, a feeling of anger grew within him. He shrugged his shoulders. 'Dead . . . is death the answer? If it were me . . .' he muttered with hatred.

'Your bath is ready, Sir,' said the servant.

Once alone, Golder went over to the bathtub, stretched his hand down into the water and left it there; all his movements were extraordinarily slow and hesitant, incomplete. The cold water froze his fingers, his arm, his shoulder, but he lowered his head and didn't move, staring dumbly at the reflection of the electric light bulb hanging from the ceiling as it shone and shimmered in the water.

'If it were me . . .' he said again.

Old, forgotten memories were resurfacing from deep within his mind. Dark, strange memories . . . A whole, harsh lifetime of struggle . . . Today, riches, tomorrow, nothing. Then starting over . . . And starting over again . . . Oh yes, if he'd ever considered *that*, well, honestly, he would have been dead long ago. He sat up straight, absentmindedly shook the water off his hand and leaned against the window, holding his freezing hands towards the warmth of the sun. He shook his head and said out loud, 'Yes, honestly, in Moscow for example, or even in Chicago . . .' and his mind, unaccustomed to dreaming, conjured up the past in brief, dry little snapshots.

Moscow ... when he was nothing more than a thin little Jew with red hair, pale, piercing eyes, worn-out boots and empty pockets ... He used to sleep rough on benches, in the town squares, on dark autumn nights like these, so cold ... Fifty years later, he could still feel in his bones the dampness of the thick white early morning fog, a fog that clung to his body, leaving a sort of stiff frost on his clothes ... Snowstorms, and in March, the wind ...

And Chicago ... the small bar, the gramophone with its grating, tinny old-fashioned European Waltz, that feeling of all-consuming hunger as the warm smells from the kitchen wafted towards him. He closed his eyes and pictured in extraordinary detail the shiny, dark face of a black man, drunk or ill, slumped on a bench in the corner, who was hooting plaintively, like an owl. And then ... His hands were burning now. He carefully held them flat against the glass, then took them away again, wiggled his fingers and gently rubbed his hands together.

'Fool,' he whispered, as if the dead man could hear him, 'you fool ... Why did you go and do it?'

Golder fumbled about at Marcus's door for some time before ringing the bell: his thick, cold hands couldn't find the buzzer and hit the wall instead. When he got inside, he looked around him in a kind of terror, as if he expected to see the dead man laid out, ready to be taken away. But there were only some rolls of black fabric on the floor of the entrance hall and bouquets of flowers on the armchairs; they were tied with purple silk inscribed with gold lettering, and the ribbons were so long and wide they trailed on to the carpet.

While Golder was standing in the hall, someone rang the bell and delivered an enormous, thick wreath of red chrysanthemums through the half-open door; the servant slipped it over his arm as if it were the handle of a basket.

'I must send some flowers,' Golder thought.

Flowers for Marcus . . . He pictured the heavy face with its grimacing lips, and a bridal bouquet beside it . . .

'If you would care to wait for a moment in the drawing room, Sir,' the servant whispered, 'Madame is with . . .' He made a vague, embarrassed gesture. '. . . with Monsieur, with the body . . .'

He held out a chair for Golder and left. In the adjoining room, two voices were talking in a vague, mysterious whisper, as if at prayer; the voices grew gradually louder until Golder could hear them.

'The hearse decorated with Greek statues and a silver rail,

12

in the Imperial style, with five plumes, and an ebony panelled, silk-lined casket with eight carved, silver-gilt handles are included in the Superior Class. Then we have the Class A; that comes with a polished mahogany casket.'

'How much?' a woman's voice whispered.

'Twenty thousand two hundred francs with the mahogany casket. Twenty-nine thousand three hundred for the Superior Class.'

'I don't think so. I only want to spend five or six thousand. If I had known how much you charged I would have gone elsewhere. The coffin can be made of ordinary oak if it's covered in large enough draperies . . .'

Golder got up abruptly; the voice immediately went quiet, softening once again to a solemn whisper.

Angrily, Golder grasped his handkerchief between his hands and absentmindedly twisted and knotted it. 'It's stupid, all this . . .' he muttered, 'it's so stupid . . .'

He couldn't think of any other way to describe it. There wasn't any other way. It was stupid, just stupid . . . Yesterday Marcus was sitting opposite him, shouting, alive, and now . . . No one even used his name anymore. The body . . . He breathed in the heavy, sickly smell that filled the room. Is that him, already, he thought, horrified, or these awful flowers? 'Why did he do it?' he muttered to himself in disgust, 'Why kill yourself, at his age, over money like some little nobody . . .' How many times had he lost everything, and like everyone else just picked himself up and started again? That was how it was. 'And as for this Teisk business,' he said out loud, vehemently, as if he were imagining himself in Marcus's place, 'he had a hundred to one chance it would come off, especially with Amrum involved, the fool!'

All sorts of ideas were buzzing angrily around in his mind.

'You never know what's going to happen in business, you have to go with your instincts, change your tactics, try everything you can, but to choose death . . . How long are they going to make me wait?' he thought with disgust.

Marcus's wife came in. Her thin face with its large, beak-like nose had the sallow colour of antler-horn; her round, bright eyes glittered beneath her thin eyebrows, which sat very high on her forehead and looked oddly uneven.

She walked towards Golder with small hurried steps, took his hand and seemed to be waiting for him to say something. But Golder had a lump in his throat and said nothing.

'Yes. You weren't expecting it . . .' she murmured with a bizarre little high-pitched squeal that sounded like a nervous laugh or stifled sob. 'This madness, this humiliation, this scandal . . . I thank the Good Lord for not having given us children. Do you know how he died? In a brothel, on the Rue Chabanais, with whores. As if going bankrupt weren't enough,' she concluded, dabbing her eyes with her handkerchief.

Her sudden movement revealed beneath her black veil an enormous pearl necklace wound three times around her long, wrinkled neck which she jerked about like an old bird of prey.

'She must be very rich,' thought Golder, 'the old crow. It's always the same story: we kill ourselves working so that "the women" can get richer . . .' He pictured his own wife quickly hiding her chequebook whenever he came into the room, as if it were a packet of love letters.

'Would you like to see him?' she asked.

An icy wave flooded over Golder; he closed his eyes and replied in a shaky, colourless voice: 'Of course, if I . . .'

Madame Marcus silently crossed the large drawing room and opened a door, but it led only to another, smaller room, where two women were sewing some black material. Eventually she said, 'In here.' Golder could see candles burning dimly. He stood motionless and silent for a moment, then made an effort to speak.

'Where is he?'

'Here,' she said, pointing to a bed that was partly hidden beneath a great velvet canopy. 'But I had to cover up his face to keep away the flies . . . The funeral is tomorrow.'

It was only then that Golder thought he could make out the dead man's features beneath the sheet. He looked at him for a long time with strange emotion.

'My God, they're in such a hurry,' he thought, overwhelmed by a confused feeling of anger and hurt. 'Poor Marcus . . . How helpless we are when we die . . . It's disgusting . . .'

In the corner of the room stood a large American-style desk with its top open; papers and opened letters were scattered about the floor. 'There must be some letters from me in there,' he thought. He spotted a knife lying on the carpet. Its silver blade was all twisted. The drawers had been forced; there were no keys in the locks.

'He probably wasn't even dead when she rushed in to see what was left; she couldn't bear to wait, to try to find the keys . . .'

Madame Marcus caught the look on his face, but stared straight at him; all she did was to mutter curtly, 'He left nothing.' Then she added more quietly, in a different tone of voice, 'I'm on my own.'

'If I can help in any way . . .' Golder automatically replied.

She hesitated for a moment. 'Well,' she said finally, 'what would you advise me to do with the Houillère shares?'

'I'll buy them from you at what they cost,' said Golder. 'You do know they'll never be worth anything? The company went bankrupt. But I'll also have to take some of these letters. I imagine you expected as much, didn't you?' he added in a hostile, sarcastic way that she appeared not to notice. She simply nodded and stepped back a bit. Golder began sifting through the papers in the half-empty drawer. But he couldn't manage to overcome a sudden feeling of sad, bitter indifference. My God, what's the point of it all, in the end?

'Why did he do it?' he asked abruptly.

'I don't know,' said Madame Marcus.

'Was it over money? Just money?' He was thinking out loud. 'It just isn't possible. Didn't he say anything at all before he died?'

'No. When they brought him back here, he was already unconscious. The bullet was lodged in his lung.'

'I see,' Golder said with a shudder, 'I see.'

'Later on, he tried to speak, but his mouth was full of foam and blood. He only said a few words, just before he died . . . He was almost peaceful and I asked him, "Why? How could you do such a thing to me?" He said something I could barely make out . . . Just one word that he kept repeating: "Tired . . . I was . . . tired . . ." And then he died.'

'Tired,' thought Golder, who suddenly felt his age bearing down on him, like a heavy weight. 'Yes.'

A violent storm was beating down on Paris the day of Marcus's funeral; everyone was in a hurry to bury the dead man deep within the wet earth and then leave.

Golder was holding his umbrella in front of his face, but when the coffin went past, balanced on the shoulders of the pall bearers, he stared at it; the black fabric, embroidered with tear-shaped silver drops, had slipped away, revealing the cheap wood and tarnished metal handles. Golder turned sharply away.

Next to him, two men were talking loudly. One of them pointed to the hole being filled in.

'He came to see me,' Golder could hear one of them saying, 'and offered to pay me with a cheque drawn on the French Bank of America in New York, and I was foolish enough to agree. It was the night before he died, Saturday. As soon as I'd heard he'd killed himself, I cabled but only got a reply the following morning. Naturally, he'd cheated me. Insufficient funds. But I'm not going to let it drop, his widow will have to make it good . . .'

'Was it for a lot of money?' someone asked.

'Not to you perhaps, Monsieur Weille, not to you,' the voice replied bitterly, 'but to a poor man like me, it was an awful lot of money.'

Golder looked at him. He was a small, hunched old man, rather shabbily dressed, who stood shaking in the

17

coughing. As no one said anything,
complaining in a low voice. Someone else
laughing.

'You'd be better off asking the Madame at the Rue
Chabanais, she's the one who's got your money.'

Behind Golder, two young men were whispering behind
an open umbrella: 'The thing's a farce . . . You know they
found him with some little girls? Only thirteen or fourteen
years old . . . It's absolutely true, and on top of that . . .' He
lowered his voice.

'Who would have guessed he had a taste for that . . .'

'Maybe he was just trying to satisfy a secret desire before
dying, what do you think?'

'Trying to hide his predelictions more likely . . .'

'Do you know why he killed himself?'

Golder automatically took a few steps forward, then
stopped. He looked at the gleaming gravestones, the battered
wreaths, whipped by the wind. He vaguely muttered
something. The man next to him turned around.

'What were you saying, Golder?'

'What a mess, don't you think?' Golder said, suddenly
sounding angry and oddly pained.

'Yes, when it's raining, a funeral in Paris is never much
fun. But it will happen to all of us one day. Good old Marcus,
even on the last day we'll ever have anything to do with
him, he's arranged for all of us to die of pneumonia. If he
can see us now plodding about in the mud, it will make him
so happy . . . He was pretty tough, wasn't he? By the way,
you'll never guess what I heard yesterday.'

'What?'

'Well, I heard that the Alleman Company was going to
bail out Mesopotamian Petroleum. Have you heard anything
about that? You'd find that interesting, wouldn't you?'

He stopped speaking and pointed with satisfaction at the
umbrellas that were beginning to move in front of them.

'Ah! It's over at last, not before time. Let's get going . . .'

With their collars up, the mourners pushed each other to escape the rain as quickly as possible. Some of them even ran over the graves. Like everyone else, Golder held his open umbrella with both hands and hurried away. The storm was pounding down on the trees and gravestones, beating them with a kind of futile, savage violence.

'How smug they all look, the lot of them,' Golder thought. 'One down, and now there's one enemy less . . . And how happy they'll all be when it's my turn.'

They had to stop on the path for a moment to let a procession pass that was going in the opposite direction. Braun, Marcus's secretary, caught up with Golder.

'I have some more papers on the Russians and Amrum which will be of interest to you,' he whispered. 'Everyone seems to have been stabbing everyone in the back . . . Not a very nice business, Monsieur Golder.'

'You think so, young man?' replied Golder, with a sarcastic look on his face. 'No, not very nice. Well, bring everything to me at the train station at six o'clock, to the train for Biarritz.'

'Are you going away, Monsieur Golder?'

Golder took a cigarette and crushed it between his fingers.

'Are we going to be here all night, for God's sake?'

The line of black cars was still filing past, relentless and slow, blocking the way.

'Yes, I'm going away.'

'You'll have wonderful weather. How is Mademoiselle Joyce? She must be even more beautiful now . . . You'll be able to have a rest. You look nervous and tired.'

'Nervous,' grumbled Golder, suddenly furious, 'no, thank God! Where do you get such rubbish? Now Marcus was another story . . . He was as jittery as a woman . . . And you can see where it got him . . .'

He pushed his way past two undertakers in shiny, dripping hats who were walking in the middle of the path, and fled, cutting through the funeral procession to get outside the gates.

It wasn't until he was in the car that he remembered he hadn't paid his respects to the widow. 'Oh, she can go to hell!' He tried in vain to light his cigarette, but the rain had soaked it, so he spat the crushed tobacco out of the window. He huddled in the corner and closed his eyes as the car pulled away.

Golder dined quickly, drank some of the heavy Burgundy he liked, then smoked for a while in the corridor. A woman bumped into him as she passed by and smiled, but he looked away, indifferent. She was one of those little sluts from Biarritz . . . She disappeared. He went back into his compartment.

'I'm going to sleep well tonight,' he thought. He suddenly felt exhausted; his legs were heavy and painful. He raised the blind and looked out blankly at the rain streaming down the dark windows. The drops of water ran into each other forming little, wind-whipped rivers, like tears . . . He undressed, got into bed and buried his face deep in the pillow. He had never felt so exhausted. He stretched his arms out with difficulty; they were stiff, heavy . . . The berth was narrow . . . even narrower than usual, it seemed. 'A bad choice of compartment, of course . . . the idiots,' he thought vaguely. He could feel his body jolt as the wheels beneath him revolved with a heart-rending screech. The heat was suffocating. He turned over his pillow, then turned it again; he was burning up. He punched it down with his fist, angrily. It was so hot . . . It would be better to open the window. But the wind was blowing furiously. In a flash, all the letters and newspapers on the table flew into the air. He swore, closed the window again, pulled the blind down, switched off the light.

The air was heavy and smelled of coal mixed with a faint

21

odour of eau de toilette. It made him feel sick. Instinctively, he tried to breathe more deeply, as if to force the heavy air into his lungs, but they rejected it, could not absorb it; it remained in his throat, choking him, like when you try to force food into a nauseous stomach . . . He kept coughing. It was irritating . . . Worst of all, it was preventing him from sleeping. 'And I'm so terribly tired,' he murmured, as if complaining to some invisible companion.

He turned on to his back, then rolled slowly over on to his side again, pushing himself up on his elbows. He gave a deliberate, hard cough in an attempt to shrug off the unbearable feeling of heaviness high in his chest, in his throat. It didn't work; he felt even worse. He yawned with difficulty, but a sharp spasm turned the yawn into a painful fit of choking. He stretched his neck, moistened his lips. Perhaps his head was too low? He reached for his overcoat, rolled it up, slipped it under the pillow, then pulled himself into a sitting position. It was worse. His lungs felt as if they were swelling up. And . . . it was strange . . . He had pains . . . yes, pains in his chest, in his shoulder, around his heart . . . Suddenly, a shiver ran down his spine. 'What's happening?' he whispered anxiously. Then he said bravely, 'No, it's nothing, it will stop. It's nothing . . .' and he realised he was talking out loud, talking to himself. He braced himself, put all his effort into inhaling deeply, but it was no use. He couldn't breathe. He felt an invisible weight crushing his chest. He threw off the covers, the sheet, opened his nightshirt. 'What's going on?' he panted, 'What's wrong with me?' The thick, black darkness bore down on him like a stone. That's what was suffocating him, yes, that was it . . . He reached out his shaking hand to turn on the light, but it fumbled along the wall in the dark, trying in vain to find the little lamp set in the wall above the bed. He sighed angrily, shuddered. The pain in his shoulder was becoming sharper, more insistent . . . Cunningly lying in wait, he thought, pacing about somewhere deep inside his body, in the very core of his being, in his heart, waiting for him to make the slightest movement and then it would strike. Slowly he lowered his arm; it was if he was forcing it down. Just wait . . . don't move. Whatever happens, don't move . . . He was breathing more and more heavily and quickly. The air entered his lungs with a strange, grotesque sound, like steam hissing from the lid of a cauldron; and when he breathed out, his entire chest began to convulse, filled with a hoarse, choked wheezing, like a moan, like a death-rattle.

The thick darkness flowed into his throat with soft, insistent pressure, as if earth was being pushed into his mouth, as it was into *his* . . . the dead man's . . . Marcus . . . And when he thought finally of Marcus, when he finally allowed himself to be taken over by the image, the memory of death, the cemetery, the yellow clay soaked with rain, the long roots clinging like serpents deep inside the grave, he suddenly felt such a tremendous need, such a desperate desire for light, to see familiar, ordinary things around him . . . his clothing swaying from the hook on the door . . . the newspapers on the little table . . . the bottle of mineral water . . . that he forgot about everything else. Angrily he stretched out his arm, and an excruciating pain, as sharp as a knife, like a bullet, deep and violent, shot through his chest, seemed to embed itself deep within his heart.

He had time to think 'I'm dying', to feel he was being pushed, thrown over the edge of a precipice into an abyss, a crater, as narrow and suffocating as a tomb. He could hear himself calling out, but his voice sounded as if it were coming from very far away, as if it were someone else's voice, separated from him by deep, murky water that swept over him and was dragging him down, lower and lower, into the wide, gaping hole. The pain was unbearable. Soon he fainted, which eased the pain a little, transforming it into a feeling of heaviness, suffocation, an exhausting and vain battle. Once again, he could hear someone calling in the distance, panting, shouting, struggling. He felt as if someone were holding his head under water and that it went on for centuries.

Finally, he came to.

The sharp pains had stopped. But his entire body felt wracked, as if all his bones had been broken, crushed beneath heavy wheels. And he was afraid to move, afraid to lift a single finger, afraid to call out. The slightest sound, the slightest movement would make it start all over again, he was sure of it . . . and this time, it would mean death. Death.

In the silence, he could hear his heart beating, hard and hollow; it seemed to tear at the muscles in his chest.

'I'm afraid,' he thought desperately, 'I'm afraid . . .'

Death. No, it wasn't possible, no! Couldn't anyone tell, sense that he was here, alone like a dog, abandoned, dying? 'If I could only ring the bell, call someone. No, I just have to wait, wait . . . The night will soon pass.' It had to be very late already, very late . . . He peered anxiously into the darkness that surrounded him; it was as thick and deep as before, without a glimmer of light, without even that vague halo that illuminates everything just before dawn. Nothing. Was it ten o'clock, eleven o'clock? To think that his watch was right there, the light was there, that he only had to reach out, stretch out his arm to press the alarm. It was worth the risk! But no, no . . . He was afraid to make a sound, afraid to breathe. If it happened again, if he felt his heart failing . . . and that horrible pain . . . No! The next time, he would surely die. 'But what's happening, for God's sake? What is it? My heart. Yes.' But he'd never had heart trouble. He'd never even been ill . . . A bit of asthma, perhaps . . . Especially recently. But at his age, everyone had something wrong. A bit of discomfort. It was nothing. Watch your diet, get some rest. But this! Oh, what difference if it was his heart or something else? They were only words, words that mean one thing: death, death, death. Who was it who'd said, 'It will

happen to all of us one day'? Oh, yes. Today, at the funeral
. . . All of us. And him. Those old Jews with their vicious
faces who rubbed their hands together, sniggering . . . It would
be worse for him! The dogs, the bastards! And the others
. . . His wife . . . His daughter . . . Yes, even her, he was no
fool. He was nothing more than a money machine . . . Good
for nothing else . . . Just pay, pay, and then, drop down
dead . . .

Good Lord, wouldn't this damned train ever stop? It had
been hours, they'd been travelling for hours without a break!
'Don't people sometimes make a mistake at stations and open
the door of a compartment that's already occupied? My God,
if only that would happen now!' He imagined hearing a
sound in the corridor, the door banging open, people's faces
. . . He would be taken away. . . It didn't matter where – to
a hospital, a hotel . . . Anywhere, as long as they had a
stretcher . . .

The sound of footsteps, human voices, some light, an open
window . . .

But no, nothing. Nothing at all. The train was going faster.
Long, piercing whistles filled the air, then faded away . . .
There was the sound of wheels pounding the tracks in the
darkness . . . a bridge . . . For a moment he thought that the
train was slowing down. He listened hard, gasping for breath.
Yes, they were going slower . . . slower . . . they'd stopped
. . . A shrill whistle sounded, hung for a moment over the
open countryside, and the train started moving again.

He shuddered. He had lost all hope. His mind was blank.
He wasn't even suffering any more. There was nothing now
but fear: 'I'm afraid, I'm afraid, I'm afraid', and his racing,
thundering heart.

Suddenly he thought he could make out something
shining, faintly, through the thick blackness. It was opposite
him. He strained to see. Barely a glimmer of light. Greyish,
pale . . . But nevertheless something bright, distinct, in the

darkness. He waited. It expanded, became clearer, spread, like a pool of water. It was the glass of the window, the window. It was dawn. The darkness was fading, becoming less dense, more fluid. He felt as if an enormous weight was lifting from his chest. He was breathing. This lighter air glided, flowed into his lungs. With infinite care, he moved his head. Cool air swept across his damp brow. Now he could make out shapes around him, outlines. His hat, for example, that had fallen on the floor . . . The water bottle . . . Maybe he could reach the glass, drink a bit? He stretched out his hand. He felt no pain, nothing. His heart pounding, he moved his wrist. Still nothing. His hand felt its way to the table, held the glass. It had water in it, thank God; he never would have been able to lift the bottle. He raised his head slightly, put the glass to his lips and drank. How wonderful it was . . . The flow of cool water across his lips, moistening his dry, swollen tongue, his throat. With the same care, he put the glass down, moved back a bit, waited. His chest still hurt. But less, a lot less, as each moment passed. It was more like a kind of neuralgia in his bones. Maybe it wasn't so serious after all . . .

Perhaps he could open the blind. All he had to do was press a button. Trembling, he stretched out his hand again. The blind suddenly sprang up. It was day. The air was white, cloudy and thick as milk. Slowly, with measured, methodical movements, he picked up his handkerchief, wiped his cheeks and lips. Then he put his face against the window. The cold of the glass felt wonderful as it ran through his whole body. He looked out at the hills where the grass was gradually recovering its greenness, at the trees . . . Far away in the distance he could see lights glowing faintly in the dawn fog. A railway station. Should he call someone? It would be easy. But how strange that it should have gone away like that . . . Though it did prove that it wasn't anything serious, at least not as serious as he had feared. An anxiety attack perhaps?

Still, he couldn't ignore it, he'd have to see a doctor. But it didn't have to be his heart. Asthma, maybe? No, he wouldn't call anyone. He looked at his watch. Five o'clock. Come on now, just wait a bit. No need to get all worked up like this. It was his nerves. Braun had been right, the little crook ... Cautiously, he probed the spot beneath his breast as if it were an open wound. Nothing. His heartbeat, however, was strange, irregular. So what, it would pass. He was tired. If he could just sleep for a while, that would surely fix things. Just to be oblivious ... No more thinking. No more remembering. He was absolutely exhausted. He closed his eyes.

He was already half asleep when, suddenly, he sat up. 'That's it,' he said out loud. 'I see it now ... It's Marcus. But why? Why?' At that moment he felt he could see within himself with extraordinary lucidity. Was it ... a kind of remorse? 'No, it's not my fault.' Then he added more quietly, more angrily: 'I have nothing to regret.'

He fell asleep.

Golder spotted the chauffeur standing at the door of a new car; he suddenly remembered that his wife had sold the Hispano.

'It's a Rolls now, of course,' he grumbled as he shot a look of hostility at the dazzling white car. 'I wonder what she'll have to have next.'

The chauffeur stepped forward to take his overcoat from him, but Golder stayed where he was, peering through the car's open window, trying to see if anyone was inside. Hadn't Joyce come? He took a few hesitant steps forwards to take a final hopeful but humble look at the dark corner where he imagined he would see his daughter with her light dress, her golden hair. But the car was empty. He got in slowly, then shouted, 'Get going, for God's sake. What are you waiting for?'

The car sped off. Golder sighed.

His daughter . . . Every time he came back from a trip, he looked for her in the crowd, in spite of himself. She was never there, and yet he continued to expect her with the same humiliating, tenacious and vain sense of hope.

'She hasn't seen me in four months,' he thought. He felt deeply hurt; he didn't deserve this, and yet his daughter so often aroused this very feeling within him. He felt it grasp his heart, as sharp and agonising as physical pain. 'Children . . . They're all the same . . . and they're the reason we live.

It's for them that we keep working. Not like my own father, no ... At thirteen, get the hell out, fend for yourself ... That's what they all deserve.'

He took off his hat, slowly wiped his hand across his forehead to remove the dust and sweat, then stared out of the window. But there were too many people, too much shouting, sun, wind. The short Rue Mazagran was so crowded that the car couldn't move; a young boy stuck his face against the car window as it passed by. Golder leaned back into the corner and pulled up the collar of his coat. Joyce ... Where was she? Who was she with?

'I'm going to give her what for,' he thought bitterly. 'This time, I'm going to tell her off about it. "Whenever you need money, it's 'Dearest Dad, Daddy, Darling', but not the slightest sign of affection, of ..."' He stopped himself with a weary gesture of his hand. He knew very well that he wouldn't say a thing ... What was the point? And after all, she was still at the age when girls were silly and insensitive. A little smile played at the corners of his mouth, then quickly disappeared. She was only eighteen.

They had crossed Biarritz, passed the Hôtel du Palais. He gazed coldly at the sea; it was choppy, despite the fine weather, with enormous waves. The dazzling green hurt his eyes; he shaded them with his hand and turned away. It was only fifteen minutes later, when they were on the road past the golf course, that he finally leaned forward and looked at his house in the distance. He only came here in between trips, to spend a week or so, as if he were a stranger, but every year he loved it more and more. 'I'm making myself old. Before it wasn't a problem ... hotels, sleeping compartments ... But now it's all so tiring ... It's a beautiful house ...'

He had bought the property in 1916 for one million five hundred thousand. Now it was worth fifteen million. The house was made of stone, as white and heavy as marble. A beautiful, imposing house ... When he saw its outline against the sky, with its balconies, its gardens – still slightly bare, for the sea winds prevented the young trees from growing quickly, but striking and magnificent nevertheless – a look of tenderness and pride spread across Golder's face. 'A very good investment,' he sighed deeply.

'Drive faster, Albert, faster,' he shouted impatiently.

Down below, he had a clear view of the rose-covered arches, the tamarind trees, the rows of cedars leading down to the sea.

'The palm trees have grown . . .'

The car stopped in front of the steps, but only the servants came out to greet him. He recognised Joyce's little chambermaid who was smiling at him.

'Is there no one at home?' he asked.

'No, Monsieur, Mademoiselle will be coming home for lunch.'

He didn't ask where she was. What was the point?

'Bring me the post,' he said sharply.

He took the packet of letters and telegram and began to read them as he climbed the stairs. On the landing, he hesitated for a moment between two identical doors. The servant, who had followed him with the suitcase, pointed to one of the bedrooms.

'Madame told me to put Monsieur in this room. His own room is being used.'

'Fine,' he said, indifferent.

Once in the room, he sat down on a chair, with the weary, blank look of a man who has just arrived at a hotel in some unfamiliar city.

'Is Monsieur going to have a rest?'

Golder shuddered and stood up with great effort.

'No, it's not worth it.'

'If I go to bed,' he was thinking, 'I'll never get up again.'

Nevertheless, when he'd washed and shaved, he felt better; there was just a slight, persistent trembling in his fingers. He looked at them. They were as white and swollen as a corpse.

'Are there many people staying?' he asked with difficulty.

'Monsieur Fischl, His Imperial Highness and Count Hoyos . . .'

Golder silently bit his lip.

'Which Highness have they invented now? These damned women . . . And Fischl,' he thought, annoyed, 'why Fischl, in the name of . . . and Hoyos . . .'

But Hoyos was inevitable.

He went slowly downstairs and headed for the terrace. A large purple awning was stretched across it at the hottest time of the day. Golder stretched out on a chaise longue and closed his eyes. But the sun penetrated the canvas and flooded the terrace with a strange red light. Golder fidgeted nervously.

'That colour . . .' he murmured, 'it must be one of Gloria's idiotic ideas. What does it remind me of? Something terrifying. Oh, yes . . . How had she put it, that old witch? "His mouth was full of foam and blood."' He shuddered. Sighing, he turned his painful head from side to side on the fine linen and lace cushions that were already crumpled and damp from his sweat. Then, suddenly, he fell asleep.

When Golder woke up it was already after two o'clock, but the house seemed empty.

'Nothing's changed,' he thought.

With a kind of grim humour, he imagined Gloria coming towards him up the path as he had seen her so many times before: teetering because the heels on her shoes were too high, her hand shading her aging painted face, her make-up melting in the dazzling sunlight . . . 'Hello, David,' she would say, 'How's business?' and then 'How are you?', but only the first question required a reply. Later on, the brilliant Biarritz crowd would invade the house. Those faces . . . It made him sick to think of them. All the crooks, the pimps, the old whores on earth . . . And he was the one paying for that lot to eat, drink and get sloshed all night. Bunch of greedy dogs . . . He shrugged his shoulders. What could he do about it? In the past, he had found it amusing, flattering even. 'The Duke of . . . Count . . . Yesterday, the Maharajah was at my house . . .' Filth. The older and sicker he got, the more tiresome he found people and the racket they made, the more tiresome his family and even life.

He sighed, knocked on the window behind him to call the butler who was laying the table, and gestured to him to raise the blinds. The sun blazed down on the garden and the sea. Someone called out: 'Hello, Golder!'

He recognised Fischl's voice and slowly turned round without replying. Why did Gloria have to invite *him* of all people? Golder looked with a kind of hatred at Fischl, as if at a cruel caricature. Fat little Jew ... He had a comical, vile and slightly sinister air as he stood in the doorway with his red hair, ruddy complexion and bright, knowing eyes behind thin gold spectacles. His stomach stuck out, his legs were short, skinny and misshapen. In his killer's hands, he calmly held a porcelain bowl of fresh caviar against his chest.

'Golder, my friend, are you staying long?'

Fischl walked over and took a chair, placing the half-empty bowl on the ground.

'Are you asleep, Golder?'

'No,' Golder grumbled.

'How's business?'

'Bad.'

'*I'm* doing very well,' said Fischl, folding his arms around his stomach with difficulty. 'I'm very happy.'

'Oh, yes. That pearl fishing business in Monaco ...' Golder sniggered. 'I thought they'd thrown you in jail ...'

Fischl gave a long, good-humoured laugh.

'Absolutely, I was taken to court ... But, as you can see, it didn't end up as badly as usual. Austria, Russia, France ...' he counted off on his fingers, 'I've been in prison in three countries. I hope that's the end of it now, that they'll leave me in peace ... They can all go to hell, I don't want to work any more. I'm old.'

He lit a cigarette. 'What was the Stock Market like yesterday?'

'Bad.'

'Do you know what the Huanchaca shares were selling at?'

'One thousand three hundred and sixty- five,' Golder said, rubbing his hands together. 'You really got screwed there, didn't you?'

He wondered suddenly why he was so happy to see the

man lose money. Fischl had never done anything to him. 'It's strange how I can't bear him,' he thought.

But Fischl just shrugged his shoulders. '*Iddische Glick*,' he said in Yiddish.

'He must be rolling in it again, the pig,' thought Golder. (He knew how to recognise the inimitable, telling little tremor in a man's voice that gives away his emotion even if his words appear indifferent.) 'He doesn't give a damn . . .'

'What are you doing here?' he grumbled.

'Your wife invited me . . . Hey, listen . . .'

He walked over to Golder, automatically lowering his voice. 'There's a business I know about that will interest you . . . Have you ever heard of the El Paso silver mines?'

'No, thank God,' Golder interjected.

'There are millions to be made there.'

'There are millions to be made everywhere, but you have to know how to make them.'

'You're wrong to refuse to do business with me. We're made for each other. You're intelligent, but you lack daring, you're not willing to take chances, you're afraid of the law. Don't you think?'

He laughed, pleased with himself.

'As for me, I'm not interested in run of the mill stuff – buying, selling . . . But to get something going, to create something – a mine in Peru, for example – when you don't even know where it is . . . Listen, I started something like that two years ago. When I bought the shares, they hadn't even turned over a shovelful of earth. Then the American investors jumped in. Whether you believe me or not, I'm telling you that within two weeks the land was worth ten times what I'd paid. I sold my shares for a huge profit. When business works like that, it's pure poetry.'

Golder shrugged his shoulders. 'Not really.'

'Whatever you say. You'll regret it. There's nothing fishy about this one.'

He smoked for a while in silence. 'Tell me . . .'

'What?'

He looked at Golder, narrowing his eyes. 'Marcus . . .'

But the aged face remained blank; there was a mere twitch of a muscle in one corner of his mouth. 'Marcus? He's dead.'

'I know,' Fischl said quietly, 'but why?' He lowered his voice even further. 'What did you do to him, you old Cain?'

'What did *I* do to him?' Golder repeated. He looked away. 'He wanted to cheat old man Golder,' he said abruptly, angrily, as his hollow ashen cheeks blushed suddenly, 'and that's dangerous . . .'

Fischl laughed. 'You old Cain,' he repeated smugly, 'but you're right. As for me, well, I'm too nice.'

He stopped speaking; he'd heard something.

'Here comes your daughter, Golder.'

'Is Dad here?' shouted Joyce. Golder could hear her laughing. Instinctively he closed his eyes, as if to listen for longer. His daughter . . . What a lovely voice, what a radiant laugh she had. 'Like gold,' he thought, feeling indescribable pleasure.

Nevertheless, he didn't move, made not a single sign of going towards her, and when she appeared, leaping on to the terrace in that light, quick way she had that showed her knees beneath her short dress, all he did was to say ironically, 'So you're home? I didn't expect you back so soon . . .'

She jumped on him and kissed him, then fell back on to the chaise longue and stretched herself out, crossing her arms beneath her neck and laughing as she looked at him through the long lashes of her half-closed eyes.

Almost against his will, Golder slowly reached out his hand and placed it on her golden hair; it was moist, tangled from the sea. Though he seemed barely to be looking at her, his piercing eyes registered every change in her features, every line, every movement her face made. How she had grown . . . In just four months, she had become more beautiful, more of a woman. He was annoyed to see she was using more make-up. God knows she didn't need to, at eighteen, with her lovely fair skin and her delicate, flower-like lips, which she painted a deep blood-red. Such a shame. 'Foolish girl,' he sighed, then added, 'You're growing up . . .'

'And growing beautiful, I hope?' she exclaimed, sitting up

36

abruptly then settling herself again with her legs tucked under her and her hands on her knees. She stared at him with her large, dark eyes; they sparkled with that haughty, arrogant look he so hated, the look of a woman who has been loved and desired her whole life. What was extraordinary was that, in spite of that look, in spite of the make-up and the jewellery, she had retained the wild laughter and the gauche, almost brutal gestures of extreme youth, with its light, intense grace. 'It won't last,' he thought.

'Get down, Joyce, you're annoying me . . .'

She lightly stroked his hand. 'I'm happy to see you, Dad . . .'

'So you need money?'

She saw that he was smiling and nodded. 'Always . . . I don't know where it goes. It seems to run through my fingers . . .' she spread her fingers out and laughed, 'like water. It's not my fault . . .'

Two men were coming up from the garden. Hoyos and a very handsome boy of twenty with a thin, pale face, Golder didn't recognise him.

'That's Prince Alexis of . . .' Joyce quickly whispered in his ear, 'you have to call him Your Imperial Highness.'

She jumped down, then leapt on to the balustrade and straddled it, calling out, 'Alec, come here! Where were you? I waited for you all morning, I was furious . . . This is Dad, Alec . . .'

The young man went up to Golder, greeted him with a kind of arrogant shyness, then went over to Joyce.

'And where did that little gigolo come from?' asked Golder, as soon as he was out of earshot.

'He's good-looking, isn't he?' Hoyos murmured, nonchalantly.

'Yes,' grumbled Golder, then repeated impatiently, 'I asked you where he came from.'

'He's from a good family,' Hoyos said, looking at him and

smiling. 'He's the son of that poor Pierre de Carèlu who was assassinated in 1918. He's the nephew of King Alexander, his sister's son.'

'He looks like a gigolo,' said Fischl.

'He probably is. Did anyone say he wasn't?'

'Anyway, he's with old Lady Rovenna.'

'Just her? Such a nice young man? I'm surprised . . .'

Hoyos sat down and stretched out his long legs, carefully placing his pince-nez, fine handkerchief, newspaper and books on the wicker table. The way in which his long fingers delicately touched each object, as if he were caressing it, irritated Golder deeply, and had done for years . . . Hoyos slowly lit a cigarette. It was only then that Golder noticed how the skin on the hand holding the gold lighter was all creased – soft and wrinkled like a withered flower. It was strange to think that even Hoyos, that handsome cavalier, had grown old. He must be almost sixty. But he was still as good looking as ever, suave and slim, with his small, proud head, his silvery hair, his strong body, flawless face and large, hooked nose. His nostrils flared with passion and life.

Fischl indicated Alec with a sullen shrug of the shoulders. 'They say he prefers men. Is it true?'

'Not for the moment, in any case,' murmured Hoyos. He stared at Joyce and Alec with a sardonic look on his face. 'He's so young, people don't know what they like at that age . . . Say, Golder, you do realise that Joyce has got it into her head that she's going to marry him, don't you?'

Golder didn't reply. Hoyos gave a little snigger.

'What did you say?' asked Golder sharply.

'Nothing. I was just wondering . . . Would you let Joyce marry a boy like that who's as poor as a church mouse?'

Golder pursed his lipts. 'Why not?' he said finally.

'Why not?' Hoyos repeated, shrugging his shoulders.

'She'll be rich,' Golder mused, 'and anyway, she knows how to handle men. Just look at her . . .'

38

They both fell silent. Joyce, straddling the balustrade, was talking to Alec; she spoke quickly and softly. Every now and then, she slid her hands through her short hair, pushing it back nervously. It looked as if she was in a bad mood.

Hoyos got up and quietly walked towards them, winking. His dark, beautiful eyes were extraordinarily bright beneath his thick eyebrows, and streaked with deep silver, like some rare fur. Joyce was whispering: 'We could take the car if you like and go to Spain; I want to make love in Spain . . .'

Laughing, she brought her lips up close to Alec's mouth. 'Would you like that? Well, would you?'

'And what about Lady Rovenna,' he objected, half-smiling.

Joyce clenched her fists. 'That old woman of yours. I hate her! No, you'll go away with me, do you hear? You have no shame. Look . . .'

She leaned forward and discreetly showed him a little bruise just above her eyelid. 'Look at what you did . . .'

She noticed Hoyos standing behind her.

He gently stroked her hair. 'Listen, *chica,*' he murmured:

> *Oh Mama, I want to die of love,*
> *She shouted and cried out loud,*
> *My girl, this is your very first love,*
> *And the first is best of all.*

Joyce clasped her beautiful arms together, laughed and said, 'Isn't love wonderful?'

When Gloria got home, it was nearly three o'clock in the afternoon. They were all there: Lady Rovenna, in a pink dress, Daphne Mannering, one of Joyce's friends, with her mother and the German gentleman who kept them, the Maharajah, his wife, his mistress and his two daughters, Lady Rovenna's son and Maria-Pia, a tall, dark-haired dancer from Argentina who had sallow skin as rough and scented as an orange.

The meal was served. It was drawn-out and magnificent. At five o'clock it finished, and more visitors arrived. Golder, Hoyos, Fischl and a Japanese General started playing bridge.

They played until evening. It was eight o'clock when Gloria sent her chambermaid to tell Golder that they were invited out to dinner at the Miramar.

Golder hesitated, but he felt better; he went up to his room, changed, then, once he was ready, went in to see Gloria. She was standing in front of an enormous, three-panelled mirror finishing getting dressed; the chambermaid, kneeling in front of her, was having difficulty fitting her shoes. Slowly Gloria turned towards him; her aging face was so covered in make-up that it looked like an enamelled plate.

'David, I've hardly seen you for five minutes today,' she murmured reproachfully. 'You're always playing cards . . . How do I look? I won't kiss you – my make-up's all done . . .' She

40

stretched out her hand to him; it was petite and beautiful, weighed down by enormous diamonds. Then she carefully smoothed down her short red hair.

Her full cheeks looked as if they had been inflated from inside, and were faintly lined with broken veins; her exquisite blue eyes were pale and severe.

'I've lost weight, haven't I?' she said. She smiled, and he could see the gold fillings shining in the teeth at the back of her mouth.

'Well, David, haven't I?' she repeated.

She twirled around slowly, so he could see her better, proudly arching her body. It had remained very beautiful: her shoulders, arms and high, firm breasts were extraordinarily striking, despite her age, and had retained the hard brilliance of marble. But her neck was lined, and her face sagged. This, together with her dark-pink rouge, which became purplish beneath the lights, gave her an air of decrepitude that was both sinister and comical.

'Can you see, David, how much slimmer I am? I lost five kilos in a month, didn't I Jenny? I have a new masseur now. A black man, of course . . . They're the best. All the women here are mad about him. He made that fat old Alphand simply melt away. Do you remember her? She's become as svelte as a young girl. He's quite expensive though . . .'

She stopped talking: her lipstick had smudged at the corner of her mouth. Slowly she dabbed it away and patiently redrew on to her aging, shapeless lips the pure, clean arch that the years had wiped away.

'You have to admit that I hardly look like an old woman,' she said, with a little satisfied laugh. But he was gazing at her without actually seeing her. The chambermaid brought in a jewellery box. Gloria opened it and pulled out a tangle of bracelets that had lain jumbled together in the box like bits of thread at the bottom of a sewing basket.

'Stop fiddling with that, David. . .' she continued, irritated. He was absentmindedly toying with a magnificent shawl that was spread out on the settee, an enormous piece of gold and purple silk embroidered with scarlet birds and large flowers.

'David . . .'

'What?' said Golder grumpily.

'How's business?'

Her gaze suddenly changed as a piercing look flashed like lightning between her long eyelashes, heavy with mascara.

Golder shrugged his shoulders.

'So-so,' he said finally.

'What do you mean "so-so"? You mean, not good? David, I'm talking to you!'

'Not too bad,' he said, half-heartedly.

'Darling, I need some money.'

'Again?'

Gloria angrily tore off a bracelet that wasn't closing properly and threw it towards the table. It fell on the floor and she kicked it away. 'What do you mean "Again"?' she shouted. 'You simply cannot imagine how much you annoy me when you say things like that. Come on, tell me. What do you mean? Don't you realise how expensive everything is? Your precious Joyce, for starters! Oh, money burns a hole in that girl's pocket . . . And do you know what she says to me when I dare to make the slightest criticism? "Dad will pay." And she's right – you've always got money for her! I'm the only one who doesn't matter. Do you think I can live on thin air, well, do you? What's gone wrong this time, is it Golmar?'

'Golmar! That went wrong long ago . . . If we were counting on Golmar . . .'

'But you do have something lucrative in the works?'

'Yes.'

'What?'

'Oh, you really are tedious,' Golder shouted. 'This

obsession you have with interrogating me about business! You never stop! You don't understand a thing about business and you know it. You women can all go to hell! What exactly are you worried about? I'm still here, aren't I?' He made an effort to calm down: 'You have a new necklace, I see. Let's have a look.'

She took the pearls and warmed them in her hands for a moment, as if they were wine.

'They're fabulous, aren't they? I know you're going to criticise me for spending too much money, but these days jewellery is the best investment. And it was a bargain. Guess how much they were? Eight hundred thousand, darling. That's nothing, right? Just look at the emerald on the clasp, that alone is worth a fortune, isn't it? Look at the colour, the size! And as for the pearls . . . OK, some of them are uneven, but what about those three at the front! You can get such amazing bargains. The sluts around here will sell anything for cash. If only you would give me more money . . .'

Golder bit his tongue.

'There was one young girl,' she continued, 'whose lover lost a fortune gambling; he was just a boy. She was going crazy, she wanted to sell me her fur coat, a magnificent chinchilla. When I tried to bargain with her she came here sobbing. I still said no. I was counting on her getting even more desperate so I'd have it for a better price, but I regret it now. Her lover killed himself. So of course she'll keep the coat. Oh David! If you could just see what a beautiful necklace that mad old Lady Rovenna has bought herself! It's gorgeous. All diamonds . . . No one's wearing pearls this season, you know. I heard she paid five million. Can you believe it? I've had one of my old diamond necklaces reset. I'll have to buy five or six large diamonds to lengthen it. Needs must when you don't have the money. But God, Lady Rovenna has such amazing jewellery! And she's so old and ugly. She must be at least sixty-five!'

'You're a lot richer than I am now, aren't you Gloria?' said Golder.

Gloria clenched her teeth with a little click, like a crocodile's jaws snapping shut on its prey.

'I detest jokes like that, and you know it!'

'Gloria,' said Golder, hesitating a little, 'you know, don't you, about Marcus?'

'No,' said Gloria, vaguely; she had put some perfume on her finger and was dabbing it behind her ears and under the pearls. 'No, what about Marcus?'

'Ah, so you don't know . . .' Golder sighed. 'Well, he's dead. They've had the funeral.'

Gloria stood still, her perfume bottle poised in mid-air in front of her.

'Oh!' she murmured in a softer tone of voice. She sounded pained, almost frightened. 'How? How is it possible? He wasn't old . . . What did he die of?'

'He killed himself. He was bankrupt.'

'What a coward!' exclaimed Gloria vehemently. 'Don't you think that's cowardly? What about his wife? How delightful for her! Did you see her?'

'Yes,' said Golder with a sarcastic laugh. 'She was wearing a necklace with pearls as big as walnuts.'

'And what would you have her do?' Gloria asked bitterly, 'Give everything to him like a little fool, so he could lose it all again on the Stock Market or somewhere else, so he could kill himself two years later without leaving her a penny? Men are so selfish! That's what you would have wanted, isn't it?'

'*I* don't want anything,' growled Golder. 'I don't give a damn. Only, when I think how we work ourselves to death for you . . .' He stopped speaking, a strange look of hatred on his face.

Gloria shrugged her shoulders.

'But my dear, men like you and Marcus don't work for

44

their wives, do they? You work for yourselves ... Yes, you do,' she insisted. 'In the end, business is a drug, just like morphine is. If you couldn't work, darling, you'd be as miserable as sin ...'

Golder laughed nervously.

'Ah!' he said, 'You've got it all worked out, my dear, haven't you?'

Joyce's chambermaid quietly opened the door.

'Mademoiselle sent me,' she said to Gloria who was looking at her with cold displeasure. 'Mademoiselle is ready and would like Monsieur to come and see her gown.'

Golder immediately stood up.

'That girl is so annoying,' Gloria hissed, sounding hostile and irritated, 'and you spoil her, you do, just like an old man in love. You are a fool.'

But Golder was already on his way out.

She furtively shrugged her shoulders. 'At least hurry her up, for Heaven's sake! I wait in the car while she admires herself in the mirror. She's a real handful, I'm telling you . . . Have you seen how she behaves around men? You can warn her that if she's not ready in ten minutes, I'm going without her. And I mean it.'

Golder said nothing and went out. On the landing, he stopped to breathe in Joyce's perfume with a smile; her fragrance was so intense and persistent that it filled the upstairs rooms with the scent of roses.

Joyce recognised the heavy footsteps that made the parquet floor creak. 'Is that you, Dad?' she called out. 'Come in.'

She was standing in front of the large mirror in her brightly lit room, teasing Jill, her little golden Pekinese dog, with her foot. She smiled, tilting her pretty head to one side. 'Do you like my dress, Dad?' she asked.

She was all in white and silver. Not considering his

admiration to be sufficiently enthusiastic, she made a face
and nodded towards her strong, flawless neck and beautiful
shoulders.

'I'm not sure it's low-cut enough. What do you think?'

'Can I give you a kiss?' asked Golder.

She walked over to him, offered a delicately powdered
cheek and the corner of her painted mouth.

'You wear too much make-up, Joy.'

'I have to,' she said nonchalantly. 'My cheeks are totally
white. I stay up too late, I smoke too much, I dance too
much.'

'Naturally . . . Women are idiots,' grumbled Golder, 'and
as for you, well, you're mad to boot . . .'

'I love to dance so much,' she murmured, half closing her
eyes. Her beautiful lips were trembling.

She stood in front of him and stretched out her hands,
but her large, sparkling eyes weren't looking at him; she was
looking at herself in the mirror behind him. He smiled in
spite of himself.

'Joyce! You're even vainer than before, my poor girl!
Though, your mother did warn me . . .'

'She's much vainer than I am,' she shouted crossly, 'and
she's got no excuse! She's old and ugly, not like me . . . I'm
beautiful, aren't I Dad?'

Golder pinched her cheek and laughed.

'I should hope so! I wouldn't like having an ugly daughter
. . .' He stopped talking suddenly, went pale and placed his
hand over his heart; he panted, his eyes opening wide from
a sudden sharp pain, then he sighed and let his arm drop
. . . The pain had passed, but it had gone slowly, almost
reluctantly. He pushed Joyce away, took out his handkerchief,
carefully wiped his forehead and cold cheeks.

'Get me something to drink, Joyce.'

She called the chambermaid in the adjoining room who
brought in a glass of water; he drank eagerly. Joyce had

picked up a mirror and was humming while arranging her hair.

'Daddy, what did you buy me?'

He didn't reply. She walked over to him and jumped on to his lap.

'Daddy, Daddy, look at me, come on, what's wrong? Answer me! Don't tease me . . .'

Automatically he took out his wallet and put a few thousand-franc notes into her hand.

'Is that all?'

'Yes. Isn't it enough?' he murmured, forcing himself to laugh.

'No. I want a new car.'

'What? What's wrong with the car you've got?'

'It's boring, it's too small . . . I want a Bugatti. I want to go to Madrid with . . .'

She stopped suddenly.

'With whom?'

'Friends . . .'

He shrugged his shoulders. 'Don't talk nonsense.'

'It isn't nonsense. I want a new car!'

'Well, you'll have to do without it.'

'No, Daddy, Daddy darling . . . Get me a new car, get me one, say you will! I'll be a good girl . . . Daphne Mannering has a beautiful car that Behring gave her.'

'Business is bad. Next year . . .'

'Why does everyone always say that to me! I couldn't care less, just buy it!'

'Enough! You're irritating me,' Golder finally cried impatiently.

She stopped talking, sprang off his lap, then thought for a moment and came back to lean against him.

'But Daddy . . . if you had a lot of money, would you buy one for me?'

'Buy what?'

'The car.'

'Yes.'

'When?'

'Right away. But I don't have any money. Stop pestering me.'

Joyce let out a little squeal of delight.

'I know what we'll do! We'll go to the casino tonight . . . I'll see to it that you win. Hoyos always says I bring good luck. You can buy me the car tomorrow!'

Golder shook his head. 'No. I'm coming home right after dinner. Don't you realise that I spent the night on the train?'

'So what?'

'I don't feel well today, Joy . . .'

'You? You're never ill!'

'Oh! Is that what you think?'

'Dad,' she asked suddenly, 'do you like Alec?'

'Alec?' Golder repeated, 'Oh, that boy . . . He's nice . . .'

'Would you like to see me become a Princess?'

'That depends . . .'

'I would be called "Your Imperial Highness"!'

She went and stood beneath the bright chandelier, throwing back her fine golden hair.

'Take a good look at me, Dad. Do you think I'd make a good Princess?'

'Yes,' murmured Golder with a rush of secret pride that made his heart beat faster, almost painfully. 'Yes, a very good one, Joyce.'

'Would you pay a lot of money for that, Dad?'

'Is it expensive?' asked Golder, his rare, severe smile playing at the corner of his mouth. 'I'd be amazed . . . These days, there are Princes all over the place.'

'Yes, but I'm in love with this one . . .' A profound, passionate expression swept across her face, making her grow pale.

'You know he has nothing, not a penny?'

'I know. But I'm rich.'

'We'll see.'

'Oh!' Joyce said suddenly, 'it's just that I have to have everything on earth, otherwise I'd rather die! Everything! Everything!' she repeated with an imperious, feverish look in her eyes. 'I don't know how the others do it! Daphne sleeps with old Behring for his money, but I need love, youth, everything the world has to offer . . .'

He sighed. 'Money . . .'

She interrupted him with a happy, impetuous gesture. 'Money . . . Money too, of course, or rather beautiful dresses, jewellery! Everything. I mean it, poor Dad! I'm so madly in love with all of it. I so want to be happy, if only you knew! Otherwise, I really would rather die, I swear . . . But I'm not worried. I've always had everything I've ever wanted . . .'

Golder lowered his head, then, forcing himself to smile, whispered, 'My poor Joyce, you're mad . . . You've been in love with someone ever since you were twelve years old.'

'Yes, but this time . . .' she gave him a hard, stubborn look, 'I really love him . . . Give him to me, Dad.'

'Like the car?' He smiled soberly. 'Come on, let's go. Put on your coat and let's go downstairs . . .'

In the car, Hoyos and Gloria – covered in jewellery, and as stiff and sparkling in the darkness as some heathen idol – were waiting for them.

It was midnight when Gloria suddenly leaned towards her husband who was sitting opposite her.

'You're as pale as a ghost, David, what's wrong? Are you that tired? We're going on to Cibourne, you know . . . It might be better if you went home.'

Joyce had heard her. 'Dad, that's an excellent idea,' she called out. 'Come on, I'll take you back. I'll meet you at Cibourne later, all right Mummy? Daphne, I'm taking your car,' she continued, turning towards the younger of the two Mannering women.

'Don't smash it up,' Daphne warned in a voice made hoarse from opium and alcohol.

Golder motioned to the maitre d': 'The bill!'

He had said it automatically, but then remembered that, according to Gloria, someone else had invited them to the Miramar. Nevertheless, all the other men had quickly turned away; only Hoyos looked at him with a wry smile and said nothing. Golder shrugged his shoulders and paid.

'Let's go, Joy.'

It was a beautiful night. They got into Daphne's small convertible. Joyce started the engine and set off like the wind. The poplar trees that lined the road fell away and disappeared as if into an abyss.

'Joyce, you're mad . . .' shouted Golder, who'd gone somewhat pale. 'One night you're going to kill yourself on these roads.'

She didn't reply but slowed down a little.

As they approached the town, she looked at him with wide, wild eyes. 'Were you afraid, Dad?'

'You're going to kill yourself,' he repeated.

She shrugged her shoulders. 'So what? It's a good way to die . . .'

She placed her lips against a scratch on her hand that was bleeding. 'On a beautiful night . . . wearing a ball gown. . .' she said. 'You just drive for a while . . .. and then it's over.'

'Be quiet!' he shouted, horrified.

She laughed. 'Poor old Dad . . .' Then added, 'Well, out you get, we're here.'

Golder looked up. 'What? But we're at the casino! Oh, I see now . . .'

'We'll leave right away if you want,' she said.

She sat motionless, looking at him and smiling. She knew very well that once he saw the brightly lit windows of the casino, the silhouettes of the gamblers walking back and forth behind them, and the small, narrow balcony that overlooked the sea, he wouldn't want to leave.

'All right then, but just for an hour . . .'

Ignoring the valets standing on the steps, Joyce let out a wild cry. 'Oh Dad, I do love you so! I just know you're going to win, you'll see!'

He laughed. 'You won't have a penny of it, no matter what, I'm warning you, my girl.'

They went into the casino; some of the young women who were wandering from table to table recognised Joyce and gave her a friendly smile.

'Oh, Dad,' she sighed, 'when will *I* be allowed to play, I do so want to . . .'

But he had already stopped listening to her, and instead was looking at his cards with trembling hands. She had to call him several times. Finally he turned round sharply and shouted, 'What is it? What do you want? Stop bothering me!'

'I'll be over there,' she said, pointing to a windowseat by the wall, 'all right?'

'Fine, go wherever you want, just leave me be!'

Joyce laughed, lit a cigarette and sat down on the hard little velvet bench, tucking her legs under her and toying with her pearls. From where she was, all she could see were the crowds of people surrounding the tables: the men were silent and trembling, the women all eagerly reaching out their necks in the same bizarre way in order to see the cards, the money . . . Strange men paced up and down in front of Joyce; now and again, to amuse herself, she would lower her eyes and give one of them a long, mysterious look – feminine, passionate and seductive – that would make him stop in his tracks, almost without realising it. She would then burst out laughing, look away and continue waiting.

Once, when the crowd parted to let in some new players, she had a clear view of Golder. The sudden, strange aging of his heavy, furrowed face, greenish beneath the harsh light, filled her with vague anxiety.

'He's so pale . . . What's wrong with him? Is he losing?' she wondered.

She raised herself up, eagerly straining to see, but the crowd had already closed in around the tables.

'Damn! Damn it!' she said to herself, frowning nervously. 'What if I went over to him? No, if you want someone to win, you bring them bad luck.'

She searched the room until her eyes alighted upon a young man she didn't know who was walking past her with a beautiful, half-naked young woman. She gestured to them urgently. 'Tell me, what's happening over there? That old man, Golder, is he winning?'

'No, the other sly old fox is winning, Donovan,' replied the woman, naming a gambler who was famous in casinos all over the world. Joyce threw down her cigarette in rage.

'He has to win, he has to,' she murmured in despair. 'I

want my car! I want . . . I want to go to Spain with Alec! Just the two of us, free . . . I've never spent an entire night with him, sleeping in his arms . . . My darling Alec . . . Oh, he has to win! Please God, let him win!'

The night passed. In spite of herself, Joyce let her head fall on to her arms. The smoke was burning her eyes.

She vaguely heard, as if from the depths of a dream, someone laugh as they pointed to her: 'Look, there's little Joyce, sleeping. Look how pretty she is . . .'

She smiled, stroked her pearls, then fell into a deep sleep. A little later, she half opened her eyes; the windows of the casino were becoming a paler shade of pink.

She lifted up her heavy head with difficulty and looked around. There were fewer people; Golder was still playing. 'He's winning now,' she heard someone say. 'A while ago, he'd lost nearly a million . . .'

The sun was rising. Instinctively she turned her face towards the light, then went back to sleep. It was daytime when she felt someone shaking her; she woke up, held out her hands, then closed them over the crumpled banknotes that her father, standing over her, slid between her fingers. 'Oh, Dad,' she murmured joyously, 'so it's true! You really did win?'

He didn't move; the stubble that had grown during the night covered his cheeks like thick ash.

'No,' he said; he was having trouble articulating his words. 'I lost more than a million, I think, then I won it back and fifty thousand francs more for you. That's all. Let's go.'

He turned around and walked with difficulty towards the door. She followed him, still barely awake, dragging her large white velvet coat along the floor, her hands overflowing with banknotes. Suddenly, she thought she saw Golder stop, stagger.

'I must be dreaming . . .' she murmured. 'Has he been drinking?' And at that very moment, his large body collapsed in a strange and terrifying way: he raised both arms in the air, waved them about, then fell to the ground with a deep, dull moan that seemed to rise up as if from the living roots of a falling tree that has been struck right through its heart.

'Could you move away from the window, Madame,' whispered the nurse, 'You're in the doctor's way.'

Gloria took a few steps back without removing her eyes from the bed. Golder's heavy head was thrown back and motionless; it made a deep impression in the pillow. 'He looks dead,' she thought, and shuddered.

He seemed completely unconscious. Although the doctor, leaning over his large, inert body, was feeling his pulse, listening to his heart, he didn't move a muscle, didn't even groan.

Nervously twisting her necklace in her hands, Gloria looked away. Was he going to die? 'It's his own fault,' she muttered angrily. 'Why did he have to go and play cards? I bet you're happy now, you fool' she whispered, as if talking to him directly. 'My God, think of all the money this is going to cost! Just let him get better . . . Just let it not go on for too long. I'll go mad! What a terrible night I've had . . .'

She recalled how she had spent the whole night in this bedroom, waiting for Dr. Ghédalia, wondering at every moment whether Golder was going to die, right there, right in front of her eyes . . . It had been horrible.

'Poor David . . . His eyes . . .'

He was staring at her again, with that lost look. He was afraid of death. She shrugged her shoulders. All the same, people don't just die like that . . . 'This is just what I needed!'

she thought, secretly looking at herself in the mirror.

She made a sudden gesture of frustration and anger, then sat down, straight-backed and stiff, in an armchair.

Meanwhile, Ghédalia had pulled the sheet back over Golder's chest and stood up. He let out a vague moan.

'Well? What is it?' Gloria asked anxiously. 'Is is serious? Will he be well again soon? Will he be ill for a long time? Tell me the truth, I'm begging you, I can take it . . .'

The doctor leaned back against his chair, slowly stroked his black beard, and smiled.

'My dear Madame,' he said in a melodious voice that flowed like milk, 'I can see you're very upset. However, there's no reason to get in a state . . . Yes, I know, I know . . . His fainting like that frightened us, didn't it? Worried us somewhat . . . But that's only natural. After a week or ten days of rest, he'll be fine. He's just tired, overworked . . . Alas, we all grow a little older with each passing day, don't we Monsieur? Our arteries aren't twenty years old any more. We can't stay young for ever . . .'

'You see,' Gloria exclaimed passionately, 'I knew it all along. The least little thing and you think you're about to die. Look at him! Well, say something, speak, for goodness sake!'

'No,' Ghédalia intervened, 'no, he mustn't say a word, on the contrary! Rest, rest and more rest! We'll give him a little injection to calm his nerves, and then, dear Madame, we shall leave him in peace.'

'But how do you feel?' Gloria repeated impatiently, 'Do you feel better? David?'

He made a weak gesture with his hands, and moved his lips; she saw rather than heard him say, 'I'm in pain . . .'

'Come along, Madame, let's leave him alone,' Ghédalia said once again. 'He cannot speak, but he can hear us very well, isn't that so, Monsieur?' he added cheerfully, glancing furtively at the nurse.

He went out; Gloria joined him in the next room.

'It's nothing, is it?' she started to say. 'Oh, he's so impressionable and nervous, it's awful . . . If you only knew what a terrible night I had with him!'

The doctor solemnly raised his small, white, chubby hand. 'I must stop you there, Madame,' he said in a completely different tone of voice. 'My very first rule, which is un-wa-ver-ing, is never to allow my patients to have the slightest idea of what is wrong with them, when their illness is serious . . . But, alas, to their families I owe the truth, and my second rule is never to hide the truth from my patient's family . . . Never!' he repeated, emphatically.

'What are you saying? Is he going to die?'

The doctor gave a look that was both surprised and shrewd, as if to say, 'I can see there's no point in putting on kid gloves here.' He sat down, crossed his legs and, tilting his head slightly backwards, replied nonchalantly, 'Not imminently, dear Madame . . .'

'What's wrong with him?'

'*Angor pectoris.*' He hammered home the Latin words with obvious pleasure. 'In simple words, a heart attack.'

She said nothing. 'He could live for a long time,' he added. 'Five, ten, even fifteen years, with a careful diet and the appropriate medical attention. Naturally, he will have to stop working. Nothing must upset him or fatigue him. He needs a calm life – peace, routine, no extremes of emotion. Complete rest. At all times . . . Then, and only then, can I give you my assurances that he will survive, insofar as it is possible to give any assurances whatsoever, for this is an illness, alas, that is full of sudden surprises. We aren't gods, after all . . .'

He smiled pleasantly. 'Naturally, it is out of the question to talk to him about it now. You can see that for yourself, Madame, for he is in terrible pain . . . But in a week or ten days, we might be able to hope that the worst is over. That will be the time to give him the ultimatum.'

'But it isn't possible for him to give up work. . . ' Gloria murmured in a strained voice. 'It just isn't possible. . .' Ghédalia said nothing. 'It would kill him,' Gloria concluded nervously.

'Madame,' he replied, smiling, 'believe me when I say I have seen many cases like this. Some of the most powerful men in the world are amongst my clientele, if I may say so . . . I once took care of a famous banker (for whom, I might add, my colleagues had unanimously declared there was no hope at all . . . but that's beside the point). That gentlemen suffered from the very same illness as Monsieur Golder . . . And my verdict was exactly the same. His friends and family feared he wouldn't last long. . . Well, this great financier is still alive. It's been fifteen years! He became a passionate and highly knowledgeable collector of Renaissance silverware, and now owns a very great number of remarkable pieces, including a silver-gilt ewer believed to be the first creation of the great Cellini, a real masterpiece . . . I dare say that the contemplation of such beautiful, rare objects gives him pleasures he has never before experienced. You can be sure that after the first few weeks of inevitable restlessness have passed, your husband will also discover his . . . how can I put it? . . . his hobby. Collecting enamels, gems, taking up more worldly pleasures, perhaps? Men are just big children . . .'

'You fool,' thought Gloria. She was suddenly filled with bitter amusement at the idea of David spending his time with rare books, a medal collection, or other women . . . Good Lord, this man was an imbecile! And just how did he think they would live? Buy food? Clothes? Did he think that money grew on trees?

She stood up. 'Thank you very much, Doctor,' she said, nodding to him. 'I'll think about what you've said . . .'

'Of course, I'll keep informed of my patient's progress,'

said Ghédalia, with a little smile, 'and I think it would be better to let me be the one who explains everything to him later on. It takes a lot of tact, delicacy . . . We doctors, alas, are used to it. We heal the soul as well as the body.'

He kissed her hand and left. She was alone.

Silently she paced the long, empty landing. She knew only too well – had always known – that he had never put aside a penny for her. Everything had been spent, gone into some business venture or other . . . So what now? 'Millions on paper, of course, but cash in hand, nothing, not a penny,' she hissed angrily between clenched teeth. 'What are you worried about?' he had said, 'I'm still here . . .' The fool! Surely, at sixty-eight, you should consider the possibility of death every day! Wasn't his first obligation to make sure he had left his wife a sufficient and decent amount of money? They had nothing. Once he gave up doing business, there would be nothing left. Business . . . a river of money that would dry up . . . 'There might be a million,' she thought, 'maybe two, if we scraped the bottom of the barrel . . .' She shrugged her shoulders furiously. The way they lived, a million would only last six months. Six months . . . and to cap it all, she'd have to take care of him, a useless, bed-ridden man who was dying. 'As if I need him to live another fifteen years!' she shouted out loud, hatred in her voice. 'Really . . . for all the happiness he's given me! No, no . . .' She detested him. He was mean, old and ugly. All he really loved in this world was money, bloody money, and he wasn't even capable of holding on to it! He had never loved her . . . If he showered her with jewels, it was to make her a living symbol of his own wealth, a showcase, and ever since Joyce had started growing up, all that had been transferred to her . . . Joyce? Oh, he loved *her*, all right . . . Because she was beautiful, young, happy. Pride! He had nothing but pride and vanity in his heart! As for her, if she so much as asked for a diamond, a new ring, he would make such a scene, shouting 'Leave me alone! I haven't got any more money. Are you trying to kill me?' Other men worked as hard as him. *They* didn't consider themselves stronger or more intelligent than everyone else in the world, and at least, when they were old, when they died, they left their wives well provided for! Some women were so lucky, while she . . . The truth was he had never cared about her, never loved her. If he had, he wouldn't have had a moment's peace knowing that she had nothing . . . nothing except the pitiful little bit of money she had managed to put aside by making great sacrifices . . . 'But that's my money, mine and mine alone! If he thinks that I'm going to support him with that! No thank you. I've had it with keeping men,' she murmured, thinking of Hoyos. 'No, let him sort himself out . . .' After all, why should she tell him the truth, for Heaven's sake? She knew very well that with his obsessive Jewish fear of death, he would give everything up in a flash. All he'd think about would be his precious health, his own life . . . The selfish coward. 'Is it my fault that after all these years, he hasn't been able to make enough money to die in peace? And right now, just when his business affairs are in such a horrible mess, it would be madness . . . Later on . . . I know what's happening now, I'll keep an eye on things. That deal he was talking about starting: "something interesting" he'd called it. After he's made the deal, that will be the time. It could even prove useful, to stop him from getting involved in some other mad project . . . There will be plenty of time . . .'

She hesitated, glanced at the door, walked over to a small writing desk in the corner.

Dear Doctor, I am beside myself with worry and so have decided, after careful consideration, to have my dear patient taken to Paris as a matter of urgency. Please find enclosed, with my sincerest thanks . . .

She threw down the pen and quickly crossed the corridor to Golder's bedroom. The nurse wasn't there. Golder seemed to be asleep. His hands were trembling. She glanced in his direction, then looked around until she saw his clothes lying over a chair. Picking up his jacket, she reached into the pocket, pulled out his wallet and opened it. Inside was a single thousand-franc note, folded in four; she hid it in her hand.

The nurse came in.

'He seems calmer,' she said, nodding towards the patient.

Embarrassed, Gloria bent down and touched her husband's cheek with her painted lips. Golder let out a moan and weakly waved his hands about, as if trying to push away her cold pearls from his chest. Gloria stood up and sighed.

'It's better if I go. He doesn't know who I am.'

Ghédalia returned to the house that same evening.

'I couldn't let Monsieur Golder leave,' he said, 'without making it clear that I can accept no responsibility for him. You see, Madame, the fact is that your husband is in no condition to be moved. Perhaps I didn't explain myself well enough this morning . . .'

'On the contrary,' murmured Gloria, 'you frightened me in a way that was perhaps . . . excessive?'

She fell silent; they looked at each other for a moment without speaking. Ghédalia seemed to hesitate.

'Would you like me to examine the patient again, Madame? I'm having dinner at 'Blues Villa', Mrs. Mackay's house . . . I don't have to be there for another half hour. I would be only too happy, I promise you, to be able to make a less distressing diagnosis.'

'Thank you,' she replied grudgingly. She showed him into Golder's room, then went back into the drawing room and stood behind the closed door, listening; he was talking to the nurse in hushed tones. She moved away from the door, a dark look in her eyes, then went and leaned against the window.

Fifteen minutes later, he came in, rubbing his little white hands together.

'Well?'

'Well, my dear lady, there has been such an improvement

that I am now inclined to believe that we are dealing with an attack brought about purely by nerves . . . That is to say, not by a coronary lesion . . . It is difficult to be absolutely certain, given our patient's state of exhaustion, but I can confirm that as far as the future is concerned, I can already say it is clearly possible to be entirely more optimistic. It certainly won't be necessary for Monsieur Golder to retire for many years to come . . .'

'Really?' said Gloria.

'Yes.'

He remained silent, then said casually, 'Still, I must reiterate that in his current condition, he must not be moved. However, you will have to do what you think best. My conscience is now clear and relieved, I must say, of a great burden.'

'Oh, there's no question of moving him now, Doctor . . .'

She held out her hand to him, smiling. 'I thank you from the bottom of my heart. I do hope you will agree to forget a very understandable moment of doubt and continue to care for my poor dear husband?'

He pretended to hesitate, hedged for a moment and finally promised he would.

From then on, every day for nearly two weeks, his red and white car stopped in front of Golder's house. After that, Ghédalia suddenly disappeared. Golder's first conscious act, a little while later, was to sign a cheque for twenty thousand francs to pay for the doctor's services.

On that day, they had sat the patient up on his pillows for the first time. Gloria, her arm behind his shoulders, helped him to lean forwards while she held the open chequebook in her other hand. She looked at him surreptitiously. He'd changed so much. Especially his nose . . . It had never been that shape before, she thought: enormous and hooked, like the nose of an old Jewish money-lender. And his flabby, trembling flesh smelled of fever and sweat. She picked up the pen that his weak hand had let fall on to the bed, splattering ink over the sheets.

'Do you feel better now, David?'

He didn't reply. For nearly two weeks, all he had said was 'I can't breathe' or 'I'm in pain', mumbling in a strange, hoarse voice that only the nurse seemed to understand. He lay stretched out, eyes closed, his arms tight against his sides, as silent and still as a corpse. Nevertheless, when Ghédalia left, the nurse would lean over him to tuck in his sheets and whisper, 'He was pleased. . .' and he would raise one quivering eyelid and fix her with a long, hard stare that contained a profound expression of pleading and distress. 'He understands everything . . .' the nurse thought. And yet, even later on, when he was able to give orders, it was the same; he never asked her or anyone else what was wrong with him, how long it would last, when he could get out of bed. He seemed content with Gloria's vague assurances: 'You'll be feeling better soon . . . You're overworked . . . You should give up smoking, you know . . . Tobacco is bad for you, David . . . No more gambling . . . You're not twenty any more . . .'

After Gloria left, he asked for some cards. He played Patience for hours on end, a tray placed across his knees. His sight had deteriorated because of his illness; he wore his glasses all the time now, thick glasses with silver frames, so heavy that they were constantly slipping off on to the bed. He would fumble about looking for them, his trembling hands getting tangled in the folds of the sheets. When he had finished a game, he would shuffle the cards and start again.

That evening, the nurse had left the window and shutters open: it was very hot. It wasn't until much later, when night was falling, that she tried to put a shawl across Golder's shoulders; he pushed it away impatiently.

'There, there, you mustn't get angry, Monsieur Golder, there's a breeze coming in from the sea. You don't want to get ill again.'

'Good Lord,' Golder growled, his voice weak and breathless, hesitating on every word, 'when will everyone leave me the hell alone? When will I finally be able to get out of bed?'

'The Doctor said at the end of the week, if the weather's good.'

Golder frowned. 'The Doctor . . . Why doesn't the Doctor come to see me?'

'I think he's been called to Madrid for a consultation.'

'Do . . . do you know him?'

She could see that anxious, eager look in his eyes. 'Oh, yes, Monsieur Golder! Of course.'

'Is he really . . . a good doctor?'

'Very good.'

He leaned back against his cushions, lowered his eyes, then whispered, 'I've been ill for a long time . . .'

'It's all over now.'

'All over.'

He felt his chest, raised his head, stared at the nurse. 'Why does it hurt here?' he suddenly asked, his lips quivering.

'There? Oh . . .'

She gently took his hand and put it back down on the sheet.

'You know very well, don't you? You heard the doctor? It was an anxiety attack. Nothing serious.'

'Nothing serious?' He sighed, automatically sitting up to start playing cards again.

'So it's not my . . . heart?'

He had spoken quietly and quickly, obviously very upset, and without looking at her.

'No, no,' she replied, 'come on now . . .'

Ghédalia had given her strict instructions not to tell him the truth. Still, he'd have to be told sooner or later . . . But that wasn't up to her. Poor man, he was so afraid of dying . . . She pointed to the cards.

'Look, you've made a mistake. You need the ace of clubs here, not the king. Let me see . . . put the nine there.'

'What day is it?' he asked, without listening to her.

'Tuesday.'

'Already? I should have been in London by now,' he said quietly.

'Oh, you'll have to travel less now, Monsieur Golder . . .'

She saw him suddenly go completely white.

'Why?' he whispered in a broken voice. 'Why? What are you saying, for God's sake? You must be mad! Have I been forbidden to travel . . . to leave here?'

'Not at all,' she reassured him quickly. 'Where did you get such an idea? I didn't say anything of the sort. It's just that you have to take care for a while. That's all.'

She leaned over and wiped his face; great, heavy drops of sweat were running down his cheeks, like tears.

'She's lying,' thought Golder. 'I can hear it in her voice. What's wrong with me? My God, what's wrong with me? And why aren't they telling me the truth? I'm not a woman, for God's sake . . .'

Weakly, he pushed her aside and turned away. 'Close the window, I'm cold.'

'Would you like to get some sleep?' she asked, as she walked quietly across the room.

'Yes. Leave me in peace.'

Shortly after eleven o'clock, the nurse was woken by Golder's voice in the next room. She rushed in and found him sitting on the bed, red-faced and waving his arms about.

'Write . . . I want to write . . .'

'He's got a high fever,' she thought. She tried to get him back into bed, reasoning with him as if he were a child. 'No, no, not now, it's too late. Tomorrow, Monsieur Golder, tomorrow . . . You have to get some sleep now.'

Golder cursed her and repeated his order, trying to speak in a more lucid, calmer tone of voice.

She finally ended up bringing him his pen and a sheet of writing paper. But he could only manage to scribble a few letters. His hand was so heavy and painful, he could barely move it. He groaned and murmured, 'You write . . .'

'To whom?'

'To Doctor Weber. You'll find his address in the Paris telephone directory, over there. "Please come at once. Urgent." Then my name and address. Understand?'

'Yes, Monsieur Golder.'

He seemed appeased, asked for something to drink, then dropped back on to his pillows. 'Open the windows and shutters,' he said, 'I can't breathe . . .'

'Do you want me to stay with you?'

'No. There's no point. I'll call if . . . The telegram,

tomorrow, as soon as the post office opens, at seven o'clock . . .'

'Yes, yes. Don't worry. Get some sleep.'

He dragged himself over on his side; he was wheezing and it was agony to breathe; the pain wouldn't go away. He lay still, looking sadly out of the window. The big white curtains were billowing in the breeze like balloons. For a long time, he just listened to the tide . . . One, two, three . . . The sound of the waves crashing against the rocks of the lighthouse in the distance; then the light, rhythmical lapping of the water as it flowed between the pebbles. Silence . . . The house seemed empty.

'What is it?' he thought again. 'What's wrong with me? Is it my heart? My heart? They're lying. I know they are. You have to be able to face things . . .'

He paused, nervously wringing his hands. He was trembling. He didn't have the courage to say the word, or even think it clearly: death . . . He looked at the dark sky filling the window with a kind of horror. 'I can't. No, not yet, no . . . There's still work to do. I can't . . . *Adenoï,*' he whispered in despair, suddenly remembering the forgotten name of the Lord, 'You know very well that I can't . . . But why aren't they telling me the truth? Why?'

It was so strange. While he was ill, he'd believed everything they'd wanted him to. Ghédalia . . . And Gloria. Still, he *was* getting better, that much was true. He was allowed to get up, go outside . . . But he didn't trust that Ghédalia. He could barely remember what he looked like. And as for his name . . . It was the name of a charlatan. Gloria couldn't do anything right. Why hadn't it occurred to her to call for Weber, the most highly-esteemed doctor in France? When she'd had that attack of indigestion, she'd called him immediately, of course. Whereas for him . . . Golder . . . Anything would do for him, wouldn't it? He pictured Weber's face, his penetrating, weary eyes that seemed able to see straight into your heart. 'I'll just say to him,' he murmured, 'that I have to know, I have my work, that's all there is to it. He'll understand.'

And yet . . . What was the point, for God's sake? Why know in advance? It would happen in a flash, like when he'd fainted, there, in the casino. But for ever, then, for ever . . . My God . . .

'No, no! There's no illness that can't be cured! Come on . . . I keep saying "my heart, my heart," like some sort of idiot, but even if it is . . . With medical attention, a diet, I don't know. . . Perhaps? Surely . . . Business . . . Yes, business . . . Well, that's the worst part. But I won't always be involved in business, not for ever. There's the Teisk deal now, of course. That will have to be sorted out first. But that will only take six months, maybe a year,' he thought, with the invincible optimism of a businessman. 'Yes, a year at the most. And then, that will be that. I'll be able to rest, to live a quiet life. I'm old . . . Everyone has to stop some day. I don't want to work until the day I die. I want to enjoy life. I'll stop smoking . . . I'll give up drinking, I won't gamble anymore . . . If it is my heart, I need peace and quiet. I'll have to stay calm, not get upset, or . . .' He gave a bitter laugh as a thought crossed his mind. 'Business without stress! I'll die a hundred deaths before I finish the Teisk deal, a hundred deaths . . .'

Wincing, he turned over on to his back. He suddenly felt extremely weak and weary. He looked at the time. It was very late. Nearly four o'clock. He wanted something to drink. Feeling for the glass of lemonade that was left for him at night, he accidentally banged it against the wooden table as he picked it up.

The nurse woke up with a start and peered into the room through the partially open door.

'Did you sleep a little?'

'Yes,' he replied mechanically.

He drank greedily, handed her the glass, then suddenly

stopped to listen to something. 'Did you hear that? In the garden . . . What is it? Go and see.'

The nurse leaned out of the window.

'It's Mademoiselle Joyce coming home, I think.'

'Call her.'

The nurse sighed and went out on to the landing; Joyce's high stiletto heels were clicking on the floor.

'What's wrong?' Golder heard his daughter say. 'Is he worse?'

She ran into the room, flicked a switch, and light flooded down from the ceiling.

'I wonder how you can leave it so dark in here, Dad. It's so gloomy with just that old nightlight.'

'Where have you been?' murmured Golder, 'I haven't seen you in two days.'

'Oh, I can't remember . . . I had things to do . . .'

'Where were you tonight?'

'Saint-Sébastien. Maria-Pia gave a wonderful ball. Look at my dress. Do you like it?'

She opened her large coat. Beneath it she appeared half-naked, the pink chiffon dress so low-cut that it only just covered her small, delicate breasts; she was wearing a pearl choker and her golden hair was tousled by the wind. Golder looked at her for a long time without saying anything.

'Dad, you're acting so funny! What's wrong with you? Why aren't you answering me? Are you angry?'

She sprang up on to the bed and knelt at his feet. 'Dad, listen . . . I danced with the Prince of Wales tonight. I heard him tell Mari-Pia: "*She's the loveliest girl I've ever seen. . .*" He asked her my name! Doesn't that make you happy?' she murmured with a joyous laugh that brought out two child-like dimples in her powdered cheeks. She leaned so far over the sick man's chest that the nurse, standing behind the bed, gestured for her to go away. But Golder, who usually felt suffocated by the weight of the sheets on his heart, let her rest her head and bare arms against him without saying a word.

71

'You're happy, dear old Dad, I knew it, I just knew it,' cried Joy.

Golder's tired, closed lips grimaced in an attempt at a smile.

'You were cross because I left you to go out dancing, weren't you? But it's still me who made you smile for the first time. Say, Dad, did you hear? I bought the car! If you could only see how beautiful it is. It goes like the wind . . . You're such a dear, Dad.'

She yawned and ran her fingers through her dishevelled golden hair.

'I'm going to bed, now. I'm exhausted . . . I didn't get home until six in the morning yesterday . . . I'm worn out, and tonight I danced and danced . . .'

She half closed her eyes and played with her bracelets and hummed softly, as if in a dream, '*Marquita – Marquita – your secret desires – shine in your eyes – when you dance* . . . Goodnight, Dad, sleep well. Sweet dreams . . .'

She leaned over and gently kissed his cheek.

'Off you go,' he whispered. 'Go to bed, Joy . . .'

She went out. He listened until the sound of her footsteps faded, his face relaxing into an expression of peace. His daughter . . . her pink dress . . . She brought joy and life with her. He felt calmer, stronger, now. 'Death,' he thought. 'I'm just letting myself get depressed, that's all. It's laughable. I'll have to work and keep on working. Even Tübingen is sixty-eight. For men like us, work is the only thing that keeps us alive.'

The nurse had switched off the light and brewed some herbal tea over the small spirit lamp. He suddenly turned towards her. 'The telegram,' he murmured, 'don't bother . . . Tear it up.'

'Very well, Monsieur.'

As soon as she left, he fell into a peaceful sleep.

By the time Golder had recovered, it was already the end of September, but the weather was better than in the middle of summer, without even the slightest breeze; the sky was bathed in a light as gold as honey.

That day, instead of going back upstairs to rest after lunch as he usually did, Golder sat on the terrace and had his cards brought to him. Gloria wasn't at home. A little later on, Hoyos appeared.

Golder peered at him over his glasses without saying anything. Hoyos adjusted one of the recliners so that its back nearly touched the ground, stretched out on it as if it were a bed, and let his fingertips contentedly graze the cold marble floor.

'It's beautiful out here,' he murmured. 'Not too hot. I detest the heat . . .'

'Would you happen to know,' asked Golder, 'where my daughter went for lunch?'

'Joyce? To the Mannerings, I suppose. Why?'

'No reason. Just that she's never here.'

'It's like that at her age. Say, why did you get her that new car? She's like a woman possessed now . . .'

Hoyos raised himself up on his elbow and surveyed the garden. 'Look, there's your Joy, over there!'

He went over to the balustrade and called out, 'Hey, Joy! What's going on? Are you leaving? You're a mad little thing, you know!'

'What?' grumbled Golder.

Hoyos was laughing uncontrollably.

'She's so funny . . . My word, she's got her menagerie with her . . . Jill . . . Why not take your dolls with you too? No? But what about your little Prince, eh? Aren't you taking him, my little beauty? Look at her, Golder, she's hilarious.'

'What's that?' exclaimed Joyce. 'Is Dad there? I've been looking everywhere for him.'

She ran up on to the terrace. She was wearing her travelling coat, a little hat pulled down nearly over her eyes and carried her dog under one arm.

'Where are you going?' asked Golder, standing up abruptly.

'Guess!'

'How do you expect me to know what's going on in your silly little head?' cried Golder, annoyed, 'and answer when I speak to you, will you?'

Joy sat down, crossed her legs, looked at him defiantly and started laughing happily. 'I'm going to Madrid.'

'What?'

'Oh, you didn't know?' Hoyos interjected, 'Yes, she's decided to drive to Madrid . . . All by herself . . . That's right, Joy, isn't? You're going alone?' he murmured, smiling. 'Of course, she'll probably get into an accident on the way, she drives so fast, but that's what she wants, there's nothing anyone can do. So, you didn't know?'

Golder stamped his foot angrily.

'Joyce! Are you out of your mind? What's all this about?'

'I told you ages ago that I'd be going to Madrid as soon as I had a new car . . . Why are you so surprised?'

'I forbid you to go, do you hear me?' Golder said slowly.

'I hear you. And?'

Golder made a sudden movement towards her, his hand raised. But Joyce continued laughing, her face just a little paler. 'Dad! Now *you* want to slap me? Go ahead, I couldn't care less. But you'll pay dearly for it.'

Golder lowered his arm, without touching her. 'Go on then!' he said, the words barely audible through his clenched teeth. 'Go wherever the hell you like . . .'

He sat down and went back to his cards.

'Come on, Dad,' murmured Joyce, affectionately, 'don't be cross. I could have left without saying anything, you know. And besides, why should it upset you?'

'You're going to smash up your pretty little face, my Joy,' said Hoyos, stroking her hand, 'You'll see . . .'

'That's my business. Come on, Dad, let's call a truce . . .'

She slipped her hands around his neck and gave him a hug. 'Dad . . .'

'It's not your place to suggest a truce. Leave me alone! The way you speak to your father!' he said, pushing her away.

'Don't you think it's a little late to be teaching your pretty little girl manners?' Hoyos sniggered.

Golder banged his fist down on to the cards.

'Get the hell out of here!' he growled at Hoyos, 'and as for you Joyce, just go. Do you think I'm going to beg you?'

'Dad! You always spoil everything for me! Everything I like doing! Everything that makes me happy!' shouted Joyce, with tears of exasperation welling up in her eyes. 'Leave me alone! Just leave me alone! Do you think it's been fun around here while you've been ill? I can't take it any more. "Walk quietly, speak softly, don't laugh" . . . There's been nothing but sad old angry faces to look at. I want to get away from it all . . .'

'Go on then. Who's stopping you? So you're going alone . . .'

'Yes.'

Golder spoke more quietly. 'You don't imagine for a moment that I believe you, do you? You're taking that little gigolo. Slut. Do you think I'm blind? I know there's nothing I can do about it. What *can* I do about it?' he repeated, his voice quivering.

'Just don't kid yourself that you're pulling the wool over my eyes. The person who can pull the wool over old Golder's eyes, my girl, hasn't been born yet, you hear me?'

Hoyos put his hands over his mouth and laughed quietly.

'You are tiresome, the two of you,' he said. 'Really, Golder, there's absolutely no point making a fuss. You simply don't understand women. The only thing to do is to give in. Come and give me a kiss, my lovely Joyce.'

Joyce wasn't listening; she was rubbing her head against Golder's shoulder.

'Dad, my darling Dad. . .'

He pushed her away. 'Get off, you're suffocating me . . . And get going quickly, otherwise you'll be leaving too late.'

'Aren't you going to kiss me?'

'Kiss you? Of course . . .' He placed his lips against her cheek.

Joy watched him. He was laying out his cards; it was as if his clumsy fingers were slipping on the wood of the table.

'Dad . . .' she said, 'you know I've run out of money?'

He didn't reply. 'Come on, Dad,' she continued, 'give me a bit of cash, please?'

'Cash for what?' asked Golder in a dry tone of voice that Joyce had never heard before.

She tried to hide her impatience but she couldn't help wringing her hands nervously as she replied. 'For what? For my trip! What do you expect me to live on in Spain? My body?'

Golder suppressed a grimace.

'And you'll be needing a lot of money, will you?' he asked while slowly counting out the thirteen cards for the first row of his game of Patience.

'Well, I don't know exactly how much. Look, you're being very tedious . . . It'll be a lot, naturally, just like always. Ten, twelve, twenty thousand . . .'

'Ah!'

76

She slipped her hand into Golder's jacket pocket and tried to take out his wallet.

'Oh, stop winding me up, Dad. Just give me the money now, will you! Give it to me!'

'No,' said Golder.

'What?' cried Joyce. 'What did you say?'

'I said no.'

He tilted his head back and looked at her for a long while, smiling. He hadn't been able to say no this way for ages, with the clear, harsh tone of voice he'd used in the past. 'No,' he murmured again. He seemed to savour the shape of the word in his mouth, as if it were a piece of fruit. He slowly clasped his hands under his chin and stroked his lips with his forefinger several times.

'You seem surprised. You want to go. Go. But you've heard me, not a penny. Sort yourself out. Oh, you don't know me as well as you think, Joyce.'

'I hate you!' she shouted.

He looked down and started quietly counting out his cards again. One, two, three, four . . . But when he came to the end of the row, he became confused and started repeating in a shaky voice, 'One, two, three . . .' Then he stopped, as if he had no strength left, and sighed deeply.

'Well, you don't know me all that well, either,' said Joyce. 'I told you I wanted to go and I'm going. I don't need your bloody money!'

She whistled for her dog and left. A moment later, they heard the sound of the car shooting past on the road. Golder hadn't moved.

Hoyos shrugged his shoulders. 'She'll manage, old boy . . .'

Since Golder didn't reply, Hoyos half closed his delicate, sleepy eyes and murmured with a smile, 'You know nothing about women, old boy . . . You should have slapped her. It might have shocked her into staying. You never know with little creatures like that . . .'

Golder had taken his wallet out of his pocket; he turned it over and over in his hands. It was an old black leather wallet, worn out, like most of his personal belongings; the satin lining was torn, one of the gold corners was missing and an elastic band stopped the banknotes from falling out. Suddenly, Golder clenched his teeth and started banging it angrily against the table. Cards flew off in all directions. He continued pounding the wooden table that resounded with each thump. Finally, he stopped, put the wallet back into his pocket, got up and walked past Hoyos, deliberately pushing into him with the full weight of his body.

'Now, there's a slap for you . . .' he said.

Every morning, Golder went down into the garden and walked along the tree-lined path for an hour. He moved slowly, in the shade of the great cedars, methodically counting his steps; at the fiftieth step, he would stop, lean against a treetrunk, sniff through his pinched nostrils, and take a deep, painful breath, straining his trembling lips towards the sea breeze. Then he would start walking again, taking up the count where he left off and absent-mindedly pushing away the gravel with his cane. Wearing an old greatcoat, a woollen scarf around his neck, and a worn-out black hat, he looked strangely like some Jewish second-hand clothes merchant from a village in the Ukraine. As he walked, he would sometimes raise one shoulder, in a weary, mechanical movement, as if he were hoisting a heavy bundle of clothing or scrap iron on to his back.

On that day, he had gone out for a second time around three o'clock: it was a beautiful day. Sitting on a bench with a view of the sea, he loosened his scarf, unbuttoned the top of his coat, and cautiously breathed in. His heart was beating regularly, but there was still a continuous asthmatic wheezing as the air went in and out of his chest; the sound was sharp and faintly plaintive.

The bench was bathed in sunlight, and the garden basked in a yellowish glow, as transparent as fine oil.

The old man closed his eyes, let out a sigh that was a mixture of sadness and contentment, then stretched out his perpetually frozen hands and rubbed them gently against his knees. He liked the heat. No doubt, in Paris or London, the weather was awful . . . He was expecting a visit from the Director of Golmar; he'd called the day before to say he would be coming . . . That meant, time was up; he would have to leave. God only knew where he would need to drag himself . . . It was a shame he had to go . . . It was such a beautiful day.

He heard the crunch of footsteps on the gravel path and turned around to see Loewe coming towards him. A short, pale man, with a grey, shy, weary face, he was weighed down by an enormous briefcase, crammed full of papers.

For a long time, Loewe had been a simple employee of Golmar. Even though he had now been its Director for five years, one look from Golder was still enough to make him tremble. He hurried over, hunching his shoulders, laughing nervously. Golder couldn't help thinking of what Marcus used to say: 'You think you're a great businessman, my friend, but you're nothing but a speculator. You don't know how to find or choose the right people. You'll be alone for as long as you live, surrounded by beggars or fools.'

'So, tell me why you've come,' he asked, interrupting Loewe's long, embroiled enquiry after his health.

Loewe stopped short, sat down on the edge of the bench, sighed and opened his briefcase.

'I'm afraid . . . Let me explain . . . You'll have to listen carefully . . . But perhaps it will be too tiring for you? Do you prefer to wait? The news I have . . .'

'Is bad,' interrupted Golder, annoyed. 'Naturally. Stop making speeches, for the love of God. Say what you have to say, and clearly, if that's possible for you.'

'Yes, Sir,' replied Loewe quickly.

He was having difficulty balancing the enormous briefcase on his knees; he held it against his chest with both hands and started pulling out bundles of letters and papers that he let fall haphazardly on to the bench.

'I can't find the letter . . .' he murmured in desperation. 'Oh, yes! Here it is . . . Shall I read it to you?'

'Give it to me . . .' Golder snatched the letter from him.

He was silent as he read it, but Loewe, who was watching his every move, noticed that his lips quivered slightly.

'You see,' he said quietly, as if he were apologising.

He handed Golder some other papers.

'All the problems started at the same time, as usual . . . The New York Stock Exchange, the day before yesterday, was the final blow, so to speak. But it only aggravated things . . . You were expecting it, weren't you?'

Golder looked up sharply. 'What? Yes,' he murmured, absentmindedly. 'Where's the report from New York?'

Seeing Loewe begin rifling through his papers again, Golder angrily swept them away with his fist.

'Couldn't you have got them in order before, for God's sake?'

'I only just arrived . . . I didn't even stop at my hotel.'

'I should think not,' grumbled Golder.

'You see the letter from the Bank of England?' Loewe said, coughing nervously. 'If the overdraft hasn't been paid off within a week, they're going to start selling your collateral.'

'We'll see about that . . . The bastards! This is Weille's doing. But he won't get his hands on it for long, that I can promise you. My overdraft with them is about four million, isn't it?'

'Yes,' said Loewe, nodding. 'Everyone is very negative about Golmar at the moment, very negative. The most depressing rumours have been going around the Stock Market ever since poor Monsieur Marcus . . . And your own enemies have even gone so far as to spread the most malevolent lies about your illness, Monsieur Golder . . .'

Golder shrugged his shoulders. 'Well . . .'

He wasn't surprised to hear it. Nor was he surprised at

the effect Marcus's suicide had had. 'That must have been of some consolation to him before he died,' he mused.

'None of that,' he said, 'is anything to worry about. I'll have a word with Weille. The thing that worries me the most is New York . . . It is absolutely essential that I go to New York. Is there nothing from Tübingen?'

'Yes, there is. A telegram arrived just as I was leaving.'

'Well, give it to me for Heaven's sake!'

'WILL BE IN LONDON 28TH' he read and gave a sly smile. With Tübingen's help everything would be easy to sort out.

'Send a telegram at once to Tübingen and tell him I'll be in London the morning of the 29th.'

'Yes, Sir. Excuse me, but . . . is it true what certain people are saying?

'What are they saying?'

'Well, er, that you're the one whom Tübingen has asked to negotiate an agreement with the Soviets for the Teisk concession, and that Tübingen is buying your shares and taking you into the company? Oh, that would be wonderful, a real coup, and we'll have no trouble getting credit once it's made public . . .'

'What day is it?' Golder interrupted, making rapid calculations.

'We could still leave today . . . Four o'clock . . . No, there's no point travelling on a Saturday. I absolutely must see Weille in Paris. Tomorrow, then. Monday morning in Paris; I could leave by four o'clock and be in London on Tuesday. Then I could get a ship to New York on the 1st. If only I could avoid going to New York. No, impossible. Though I'm supposed to be in Moscow on the 15th, the 20th at the latest. It's all very tricky.'

He rubbed his hands together as if he were cracking walnuts between his closed palms.

'It's not easy. I have to be everywhere at once. Well, we'll see . . .'

He fell silent. Loewe handed him a sheet of paper covered in names and figures.

'What's this?'

'Would you please take a look? It's the salary increases for the employees. Perhaps you remember? We spoke to you and Monsieur Marcus about it last April.'

Golder frowned and looked at the list.

'Lambert, Mathias, fine . . . Mademoiselle Wieilhomme? Oh yes, Marcus's typist . . . the little slut who couldn't even be bothered to type a letter properly! I don't think so! The other one, yes, the little hunchback one, what's her name?'

'Mademoiselle Gassion.'

'Yes, that's fine . . . Chambers? Your son-in-law? Tell me, don't you think it was enough to hire that moron? He deigns to come to the office twice a week when he's got nothing better to do, and for all the work he does . . . Not a penny, you hear me, not a penny more!'

'But in April . . .'

'In April, I had money. Now, I don't. If I gave a raise to all the freeloaders, all the spoiled little rich kids you and Marcus crammed into the offices . . . Give me your pencil.'

He angrily crossed out several names.

'What about Levine? His fifth child has just been born.'

'I don't give a damn!'

'Come now, Monsieur Golder, you're not as hard as all that.'

'I don't like people being generous with my money, Loewe. It's very nice making promises left, right and centre . . . but then it's up to me to sort things out when there's not a penny left in the pot, isn't it?

He suddenly stopped speaking. A train was passing. They could hear it clearly through the still air; it was getting louder, coming closer. Golder listened with lowered head.

'Won't you reconsider?' murmured Loewe. 'Levine . . . It's difficult trying to feed five children on two thousand francs a month. You have to feel sorry for him.'

The train was moving further and further away. Its long whistle hovered in the air like a plea, like a fearful question.

'Sorry!' shouted Golder, suddenly angry. 'Why? No one ever feels sorry for me, do they? No one has ever felt sorry for me . . .'

'Oh, Monsieur Golder . . .'

'It's true. I'm just expected to pay, pay and keep on paying . . . That's why I've been put on this earth!'

He breathed in with difficulty, then said quietly in a different voice, 'Put back all the names I crossed out, all right? And make those reservations. We'll leave tomorrow.'

'I'm leaving tomorrow,' Golder said abruptly as he got up from the dining table.

Gloria trembled slightly. 'Oh . . . Will you be gone long?'

'Yes.'

'Are you . . . sure that's a good idea, David? You're still ill.'

He burst out laughing.

'Why would that matter? *I* don't have the right to be ill like everyone else, do I?'

'Oh,' hissed Gloria angrily, 'that tone you take to make yourself sound like a martyr.'

He walked out, slamming the door so hard behind him that the chandelier swayed; the glass tinkled in the silent room.

'He's nervous,' said Hoyos softly.

'Yes. Are you going out tonight? Do you want the car?'

'No thanks, darling.'

Gloria turned sharply towards the servant.

'I won't be needing the driver tonight.'

'Very good, Madame.'

He placed a silver tray with liqueurs and cigarettes on the table and went out.

Mosquitoes were buzzing around the lamps; Gloria nervously brushed them away.

'Goodness, how irritating . . . Would you like some coffee?'

'What about Joy? Have you heard from her?'

85

'No.'

She said nothing for a moment, then continued in a sort of rage, 'It's all David's fault! He spoils that girl like a mad fool, and he doesn't even love her! She just flatters his inflated ego! As if he has anything to be proud of. She behaves like a little slut! Do you know how much money he gave her the night he collapsed at the casino? Fifty thousand francs, my darling. Charming, just charming! I heard all about it. How she was practically walking in her sleep in that gambling joint, wads of notes stuffed into her hands, just like some prostitute who'd rolled an old man! But when it comes to me, it's always the same arguments, the same old story: business is bad, he's fed up with having to work for me, etc.! Oh, I'm so unlucky! But where Joyce is concerned . . .'

'But still, she is a charming girl . . .'

'I know,' Gloria cut in.

Hoyos stood up and went over to the window to breathe in the fresh evening air.

'It's such wonderful weather. Wouldn't you like to go down to the garden?'

'If you like.'

They went out together. It was a beautiful, moonless night; the large white spotlights on the terrace cast an almost theatrical light over the gravel on the path, the branches of the trees.

'Smell how delicious it is,' said Hoyos. 'The wind is blowing in from Spain, there's cinnamon in the air, don't you think?'

'No,' she replied, curtly.

She leaned against a bench. 'Let's sit down, I find it tiring walking in the dark.'

He sat down beside her and lit a cigarette. For a moment, his features were caught in the flare of the lighter: his delicate eyelids were like the withered petals of dead flowers; his perfectly shaped lips were still those of a young man, bursting with life.

'Well, now, what's going on? Are we alone tonight?'

'Were you expecting someone else?' she asked absentmindedly.

'No, not especially. I'm just surprised. The house is usually as full as a country inn when there's a fair. Mind you, I'm not complaining. We're old, my darling, and we need people and noise around us. It wasn't like that in the past, but everything changes . . .'

'In the past,' she repeated, 'Do you know how many years it's been? It's terrifying . . .'

'Nearly twenty!'

'1901. The Carnival in Nice in 1901, my darling. Twenty-five years.'

'Yes,' he whispered. 'You were just a little foreigner, aimlessly wandering the streets, in your simple dress and straw hat. But that soon changed.'

'You were in love with me then. Now, all you care about is my money. I can sense it, you know. Without my money . . .'

He gently shrugged his shoulders.

'Hush, now . . . Don't get yourself in a state. Being angry ages you . . . and I'm feeling very sentimental tonight. Do you remember, Gloria, how everything looked silver and blue?'

'Yes.'

They fell silent, as they both suddenly remembered a street in Nice, thronging on Carnival night with people wearing masks who sang as they passed by; remembered the palm trees, the moon and the shouts of the crowd in Place Masséna . . . remembered their youth . . . the beautiful night, as sensual and simple as an Italian love song.

Suddenly he threw away his cigarette. 'Oh, my darling! Enough reminiscing; it makes me feel cold as death!'

'It's true,' she said, unconsciously shivering. 'When I think about the past . . . I so wanted to come to Europe. I can't remember any more how David managed to get the money to pay for my trip. I travelled third class. I watched from the deck as the other women danced, covered in jewels. Why do we have to wait until we're old to have such things? And, when I got here, I lived in a little family-run boarding house. If no money had come from America at the end of the month, I would stay in my room with nothing but an orange for supper. You never knew that, did you? I put on a brave face. God knows, it wasn't always easy. But what I wouldn't give now for those days, those nights . . .'

'It's Joyce's turn now. It's odd how that idea both annoys and consoles me at the same time. But that's not how you feel, is it?'

'No.'

'I didn't think so,' he murmured.

She could sense by the way he said it that he was smiling.

'There's something I'm worried about,' she said suddenly. 'You've often asked me what Ghédalia said about what was wrong with . . .'

'Yes. Go on.'

'Well, it was a heart attack. He could die at any moment.'

'Does he know?'

'No. I . . . I arranged things so that Ghédalia wouldn't say anything. He wanted to make him give up work. How would we have managed? He hasn't saved any money for me, nothing, not a penny. It's just that . . . well, I didn't think he would have to leave here so soon. And tonight he looked like death. So, really, I don't know what's best any more . . .'

Hoyos was quietly clicking his fingers; he looked annoyed. 'Why did you do that?'

'I thought I was doing the right thing,' she said angrily. I was thinking of you, as usual. What would happen to you if David stopped earning money? You know very well, don't you, where my money goes?'

'Oh,' he said, laughing, 'I'd rather die than live to see the day when women stopped paying for me. There's something about being an old lover that I find wickedly appealing.'

She shrugged her shoulders impatiently.

'Oh, do be quiet! Can't you tell how nervous I am! What should I do? What would happen if I told him the truth and he dropped everything? Don't tell me he wouldn't. You don't really know him. Right now, all he cares about is his health, he's obsessed with the idea of dying. Surely you've seen him every morning in the garden, wearing that old overcoat even in the sun? Oh, my God! If I had to watch him dragging on like that for years to come! I'd sooner see him die right now! If only . . . I swear, no one would miss him.'

Hoyos bent down and picked a flower; he gently rubbed it between his fingers, then inhaled its perfume on his hand.

'How wonderful that smells,' he murmured, 'it's divine . . . The faint aroma of pepper . . . I think it's these lovely little white carnations that are planted along the edges of the flowerbeds . . . You're unfair to your husband, my darling. He's a good man.'

'A good man?' she scoffed. 'Do you have any idea how many people he's ruined, how much misery he's caused, how many suicides? It's because of him that Marcus, his partner, his friend of twenty-six years, killed himself! You didn't know that, did you?'

'No,' he replied with seeming indifference.

'Well,' she continued, 'what should I do?'

'Oh, there's only one thing you can do, my poor darling. Prepare him gently, as gently as possible, make him understand . . . I don't think he'll give up the deal he's working on at the moment. Fischl told me a bit about it, but you know that I don't really understand much about business, As far as I could work out, your husband's business affairs are in a truly terrible state at the moment. He's counting on some negotiations with the Soviets to get him back on his feet. Something to do with oil, I think . . . In any case, one thing is certain: given his current financial situation, if he suddenly dies now, you'll end up with nothing but a series of terrible debts, no money at all . . .'

'It's true,' she murmured, 'his business is in chaos; I don't think even he realizes how bad it is.'

'Does anyone know?'

'Well, no,' she said, angrily shrugging her shoulders. 'I don't think he trusts anyone, and especially not me. His business! He hides it from me as if it were his mistress!'

'Well then, you see, if he knew, if he suspected that his life was in danger, he would make provisions, I'm sure. And of course, it would be an incentive to him, as well . . .'

He laughed quietly.

'His last deal, his last chance . . . Just imagine . . . Yes, you have to make him understand.'

Both of them turned around instinctively to look at the house. On the first floor, Golder's light was on.

'He's still awake.'

'I don't want to see him,' she whispered. 'I . . . He's never understood me, never loved me. Just money, money, for as long as he's lived. He's like a robot – no heart, no feelings, nothing. I've been in his bed, slept with him, for years, and he's always been exactly as he is now: hard, cold as ice. Money, business . . . Never a smile, a caress, just shouting and endless scenes. Oh, I've been so unhappy!'

She fell silent. When she moved, the light from one of the outside lamps hanging along the path made her diamond earrings sparkle.

Hoyos smiled.

'What a beautiful night,' he said dreamily. 'The flowers smell so divine, it's wonderful. Your perfume is too strong, Gloria, I've told you before. It overpowers these poor little autumn roses. What silence . . . It's extraordinary. You can hear the sound of the sea. How peaceful the night is. Listen, there are women singing on the road. Delightful, don't you think? Those clear, beautiful voices, the night . . . I love this place. I would be so upset, truly upset, if this house were sold.'

'Are you mad?' she murmured, 'What are you talking about?'

'My God, it could happen . . . This house isn't in your name, is it?'

She didn't reply.

'You've tried so many times,' he continued, 'remember? And what did he always say? Oh, the same old song: "I'm still here. . ."'

'I really should speak to him, tonight . . .'

'Yes, that would be best, I think.'

'Right away.'

'That would be best,' he repeated.

She slowly stood up.

'Oh, this whole business is so upsetting. Are you staying here?'

'Yes, it's so beautiful . . .'

When she went into Golder's room, he was sitting on the bed working, propped up on piles of crumpled pillows; his shirt was open at the neck, the unbuttoned sleeves hanging from his bare arms. He had placed the lamp on the bed, on a tray with the remains of a half-empty cup of tea, a plate full of orange peel. Its light fell full on to his bent head, making his white hair gleam eerily.

He turned sharply when the door opened and looked at Gloria, before bending even further over his work and grumbling, 'What is it? What do you want now?'

'I need to speak to you,' she replied coldly.

He took off his glasses and slowly wiped his puffy eyes with the corner of his handkerchief. She sat down stiffly on the bed beside him, fidgeting nervously with her pearls.

'David, listen. I really must speak to you. You're going off tomorrow . . . You're not well, you're tired . . . Have you considered that if anything happened to you, I'd be all alone in the world?'

He listened to her with a cold, gloomy expression, without moving, without saying a word.

'David . . .'

'What do you want from me?' he asked finally, staring at her in that harsh, fearful, stubborn way he reserved for her alone. 'Leave me be, I have work to do.'

'What I have to say is just as important to me as your

work. You won't get rid of me that easily, I can assure you.'

She clenched her teeth in cold fury.

'Why are you going away so suddenly?'

'Business.'

'Well, I didn't think you were going off to meet one of your mistresses!' she cried, crossly shrugging her shoulders. 'Oh, do be careful, David. Don't push me too far. Where are you going? Business is really bad, isn't it?'

'Not that bad,' he murmured unconvincingly.

'David!'

She was shouting nervously, in spite of herself. She made a great effort to calm down. 'I am your wife, it seems to me that I have the right to be concerned with matters that effect me as much as they do you.'

'Up until now,' Golder said slowly, 'all you've said was, "I want money, sort it out." And I always have. And that's how it will be until the day I die.'

'Yes, yes,' she interrupted impatiently, with a hint of menace in her voice, 'I know, I know. Always the same old story. Your work, your work! Meanwhile, what would *I* be left with if you suddenly died! You've really got it sorted, haven't you? So that the day you die, when all your creditors pounce on me, I'll have nothing, not a penny!'

'If I die! If I die! I'm not dead yet! Am I? Well, am I?' he shouted, trembling all over. 'Shut up, do you hear me? Just shut up!'

'Yes, that's it,' she scoffed, 'You're like an ostrich with its head in the sand! You don't want to see or understand anything. Well, that's just too bad. You've had a heart attack, my dear. You could die at any moment. Why are you looking at me like that? Oh, you must be the biggest coward in the world. Call yourself a man? A man! Just look at this wimp. I think he's going to faint. Oh, really, don't look at me like that,' she said with a shrug. 'You could live another twenty years, the doctor said so. It's just, well, what can you do?

You have to face such things. After all, we're all mortal. Remember Nicolas Lévy, Porjès, and all the others who juggled enormous fortunes, and when they died, what was left for their widows? An overdraft. Well, that's not what I want to happen to me, do you understand? Make some arangements. To start with, put this house in my name. If you were a good husband, you would have made sure I had a proper fortune of my own long ago! I have nothing at all!'

She gave a sudden scream. Golder had punched the tray and the lamp, knocking them to the ground. They shattered on the floor; the crash of glass broke the silence of the sleeping house.

'Brute! You brute! You beast!' Gloria exclaimed. 'You haven't changed, have you? You haven't changed a bit. You're still the little Jew who sold rags and scrap metal in New York, from a sack on your back. Do you remember? Do you?'

'And what about you? Do you remember Kishinev, and that little shop of your money-lender father's in the Jewish quarter? You weren't called Gloria then, were you? Well? Havke! Havke!'

He hurled the Yiddish name at her like an insult, shaking his fist. She grabbed him by the shoulders, burying his head in her chest, to drown out his shouting.

'Shut up, shut up, shut up! You brute! You bastard! There are servants in the house . . . the servants are listening! I will never forgive you! Shut up or I'll kill you!'

She let him go, shuddering: his old teeth were savagely biting into her flesh beneath her pearls. Golder's eyes were as fierce as a mad dog's. 'How dare you,' he shouted, 'how dare you make demands! You have nothing? What about this? And that? And that?'

Furiously he grabbed at the heavy necklace, twisting it around his fingers. She dug her fingernails into his hands, but he held on. He was having difficulty breathing.

'That, my girl, that alone is worth a million! And what

about your emeralds? Your necklaces? Your bracelets? Your rings? Everything you own, everything you wear, from head to toe ... And you have the nerve to say that I haven't provided you with a fortune? Just look at yourself, covered in jewels, weighed down with the money you extorted from me, stole from me! You, Havke! When I took you in, you were nothing but a penniless, miserable girl, remember? Remember? You were running through the snow, with holes in your shoes, your feet sticking out of your stockings, your hands red and swollen from the cold! Oh, my pretty, *I* remember! And I remember the boat we left on, and the immigrants' deck ... And now, you're Gloria Golder! With gowns, jewels, houses, cars, all paid for by me, by me, paid for with my health, with my life! You've taken everything from me, stolen everything from me! Do you think I didn't know that when this house was bought, you arranged to get a two-hundred-thousand-franc kickback, you and Hoyos? Pay, pay, pay ... morning, noon and night. All my life! Did you really think that I saw nothing, that I understood nothing, that I didn't see you getting richer, fattening up your bank account at my expense, and Joyce's? Stockpiling diamonds, stocks and bonds! You've been wealthier than me for years, do you hear me, do you?'

His cries were tearing at his chest; he grabbed his throat, overcome by a fit of coughing, a horrible cough that wracked his body like a gale. For a moment, Gloria thought he was going to die. But he still had enough strength left to hiss at her, a hiss that emerged with excruciating pain from the depths of his wracked chest.

'The house ... you're not getting the house! Do you understand! Never ...'

Then he fell to the ground and lay on his back, silent and motionless, eyes closed. He had forgotten she was there. All he could hear was the sound of his breathing, the cough that shook him and wouldn't stop, gathering in his throat like a huge wave, and his heart, his old, sick heart, pounding against his chest with deep, dull blows.

The attack lasted for a long time. Then, little by little, it subsided. The cough grew weaker and fainter. He turned to look at Gloria.

'Be happy with what you have,' he whispered with effort, his voice breathless and exhausted, 'because I swear to you that you will get nothing more from me ever again, nothing . . .'

She interrupted him, in spite of herself. 'Don't try to speak. It's painful just listening to you.'

'Leave me alone,' he groaned, pushing away the hand she had stretched out to him; he couldn't bear the feel of her cold rings, her cold hands on his body.

'Look. I want you to understand once and for all. As long as I live, everything will be fine. You are my wife, I've given you everything I could. But after I die, you won't get anything. Do you understand? Nothing, my dear, except everything you've already managed to amass . . . and even that's too much. I've arranged things so that Joyce will get it all. And as for you? Not a penny. Not a cent. Nothing. Absolutely nothing. Do you hear? Do you understand what I'm saying?'

He could clearly see Gloria's cheeks turn white beneath her melting rouge.

'What are you saying?' she asked in a muffled voice. 'Are you mad, David?'

He wiped away the sweat that was running down his face and looked darkly at Gloria.

'I want, I mean for Joyce to be free, rich . . . As for you . . .' He angrily clenched his teeth. 'Not you, do you hear me, not you.'

'But why?' she asked naively, without thinking.

'Why?' repeated Golder slowly. 'Ah, so you really want me to tell you why? Very well then. Because I think I've already done enough for you. I've made you quite wealthy enough, you and your lovers . . .'

'What?'

'That surprises you? I bet you understand better now, eh?
Yes, your lovers . . . all of them. That little Porjès, Lewis
Wichmann, all the others . . . and Hoyos . . . especially Hoyos.
Him! For twenty years I've watched him parading rings,
clothing, even other women, paid for with my money. Well,
enough is enough, understand?'

When she didn't reply, he repeated, 'Understand? Oh, if
you could only see your face. You're not even trying to
pretend!'

'Why should I?' said Gloria in a kind of hiss that barely
passed through her clenched lips. 'Why should I? I've never
been unfaithful to you. You can only be unfaithful to a
husband . . . to a man who actually sleeps with you . . . who
satisfies you. As for you! You've been a sick old man for
years . . . a wreck. Maybe you don't realise, or haven't been
counting, but it's nearly eighteen years since you came near
me. And before that?'

She burst out laughing. 'And before that, David? Have
you forgotten . . .'

Blood rushed to Golder's aging face turning it almost
purple, filling his eyes with tears. That laugh . . . He hadn't
heard it in years. Those nights when he'd tried to stifle it
with his lips, in vain . . .

'That was your fault,' he whispered, as he had in the past.
'You never loved me.'

She laughed even harder. 'Loved? You? David Golder? But
could anyone love you? Do you want to leave your money
to Joyce because you think she loves you, is that it? But she
just loves your money, her as well, you fool! She's gone off,
hasn't she, your Joyce? She's left you, old, sick and alone!
But while you were close to death, she was out dancing, do
you remember? I at least had the decency to stay with you.
As for her, she'll be dancing on your grave, you fool! Oh,
yes, she loves you so much . . .'

'I don't give a damn.'

He was trying to shout, but his tormented voice stuck strangled and hoarse in his throat. 'I don't give a damn. You don't have to tell me, I already know, I know. Make money for everyone else, and then die, that's why I was put on this filthy earth. Joyce is a little slut like you, I know that only too well, but she can't hurt me, not her. She's a part of me, she's my daughter, she's all I have in the world.'

'Your daughter!'

Gloria fell back on to the bed, shaking with the shrill laughter of a mad woman.

'Your daughter! Are you sure about that? You don't know, do you, you who knows so many things? Well, she's not yours, do you understand? Your daughter is not yours at all. She's Hoyos's daughter, you fool! Haven't you ever noticed how much she looks like him, how much she loves him. She guessed a long time ago, I'll bet on it. Haven't you ever noticed how we laugh when you kiss your Joyce, your precious daughter . . .'

She stopped short. He wasn't moving, wasn't speaking. She leaned over him. He hid his face in his hands.

'David . . . It isn't true. . .' she whispered automatically. 'Listen . . .'

But he wasn't listening. He was crushing his face into his hands in shame. He didn't hear her stand up, didn't hear her pause for a moment at the door, didn't see how she was looking at him.

Finally, she went out.

Some time later, he got up and dragged himself into the adjoining bathroom. He needed something to drink. He spent a while trying to find the jug of purified water that was left for him at night, but eventually gave up. Instead, he turned on the taps of the bathtub and wet his hands and mouth. He found it difficult to pull himself upright again; his legs were shaking like an old horse who has collapsed, half-dead, and can't get up, despite being urged on by the whip.

The cool night air blew in through the open window. Instinctively, he walked towards it and looked out. But he might as well have been blind: he saw nothing. He felt cold and went back into his room.

He stepped on some broken glass, let out a muffled curse, looked indifferently at the blood flowing from his bare feet, and got back into bed. He was shivering. He pulled the covers tightly around his body, over his head, pressing his forehead into the pillow. He was exhausted. 'I'm going to fall asleep . . . to forget. I'll think about it tomorrow . . . tomorrow . . .' Why tomorrow? There was nothing he could do about it. Nothing. Hoyos . . . that filthy pimp . . . and Joyce . . . 'It's true that she looks like him!' he cried out, despair in his voice. But almost immediately, he fell silent, his fists clenched. 'She loves him so much,' Gloria had said, 'Haven't you noticed? She guessed a long time ago . . .' She knew, she was laughing at him, she was only affectionate towards him when she wanted money. 'Little slut, little . . . I didn't deserve this,' he murmured painfully, his lips dry.

He had loved her so much, been so proud of her. None of them had given a damn about him, none of them. A child of his own . . . What a fool he was! He had really believed he could possess something precious on this earth . . . To work all his life just to end up empty-handed, alone and vulnerable, that was his fate. A child! Even at forty he'd been as old and cold as a corpse! It was Gloria's fault, she'd always hated him, mocked him, pushed him away . . . Her laugh . . . Because he was ugly, heavy, clumsy . . . And at the beginning, when they were poor, her fear, her terror at having a child . . . 'David, be careful. David, listen, if you get me pregnant, I'll kill myself . . .' Wonderful nights of love they'd been! And then . . . He remembered now, he remembered it all quite clearly . . . He counted. It was in 1907. Nineteen years ago. She was in Europe, he was in America. A few months earlier, for the first time, he had earned some money, a lot of money in a construction deal. Then he had nothing again. Gloria was wandering about alone, somewhere in Italy. Now and again, she'd send short telegrams: 'Need money.' He always managed to get some for her. How? Ah, a Jewish husband always has to find a way . . .

A company was formed by some American financiers to construct a railway line in the West. A terrible region, vast empty spaces, swamps . . . Eighteen months later, all the money was gone. Everyone got out, one after the other, and he'd stepped in to take control of the business. He'd raised more capital, gone out there, stuck it out . . . Whenever he got his big, heavy hands on some deal, he didn't let go easily, oh no . . .

He'd lived alongside the workmen in a wooden hut made of rotting boards. It was the rainy season. Water dripped through the badly constructed roof and down the walls; when night fell, there was a loud whine of enormous mosquitoes from the swamp. Every day, men died, burning with fever. They were buried at night so as not to interrupt the work. The coffins would sit waiting all day long, under wet, shiny tarpaulins that rattled in the wind and rain.

And it was in that place that Gloria had arrived one fine day, with her fur coat, her painted nails, her high heels that got stuck in the mud . . .

He remembered how she went into his room, how she forced open the small, filthy window. Outside the frogs were croaking. It was an autumn evening; the sky reflected in the swamps was deep red, almost brown . . . Such a pretty sight! A miserable little village . . . the smell of moss on wood, of mud, of damp . . . 'You're mad,' he kept saying, 'What are you doing here? You'll catch a fever . . . As if I need a woman to worry about . . .' 'I was bored, I wanted to see you. We're man and wife yet we live like strangers, at opposite ends of the world.' Later on, he asked, 'Where will you sleep?' There was only one narrow, hard camp bed. He remembered how she had replied softly, 'Why, with you, David . . .' God knows he hadn't wanted anything to do with her that night. He was numb with exhaustion, work, lack of sleep, fever . . . He breathed in her perfume with a kind of fear; he'd almost forgotten. 'You're mad,' he kept saying, 'You're mad . . .' as she pressed her burning body against his and whispered angrily through her clenched teeth, 'Don't you feel anything? You're still a man, aren't you? Aren't you ashamed?' Had he really suspected nothing? He couldn't remember anymore. Sometimes, you close your eyes and turn away: you don't want to see. What's the point? Especially when there's nothing you can do anyway? And afterwards, you forget . . . That night, she had pushed him aside, with that weary gesture of an animal who's had its fill. She'd fallen asleep where she lay, her arms crossed over her chest, her breathing heavy, as if she were having a nightmare. He had got up, started working, as he did every night. The kerosene lamp burned and went black, it was raining outside, the frogs were croaking beneath the windows.

A few days later she left. That same year, Joyce was born. Of course . . .

Joy . . . Joy . . . He said her name over and over again, with a kind of hoarse, dry sob, like the cry of an animal in pain. He had really loved her, his Joy, his daughter, his little girl . . . He had given her everything, and she couldn't care less about him. She had snuggled against him in the same way a slut caresses and kisses the sad old man who's in love with her. She knew very well that he wasn't her father. Money. Money was the only thing that mattered to her. Otherwise, why would she have gone away like that? And when he kissed her, she would turn away from him, saying, 'Oh, Dad! You'll ruin my make-up.' She was ashamed of him. He was heavy and clumsy, unsophisticated . . . A feeling of wild humiliation stabbed at his heart. A hot tear dropped from his swollen eyes on to his cheek. He wiped it away with a trembling hand. Cry over her? He, David Golder? Over that little slut? 'She's gone off . . . she's left you, old, sick and alone . . .' But at least she hadn't taken any of his money this time. He remembered with sharp, savage pleasure how she'd left without a penny. And Hoyos . . . how he'd said, 'You should have slapped her.' What was the point? Refusing her money had been the best revenge. They had forgotten that the money belonged to him, and that if he wanted, they would all die of hunger, all of them . . . He said 'all of them' but he was really only thinking of Joyce. She'd get nothing more from him, not so much as, he harshly snapped his fingers, a penny. Ah, they had forgotten who he was. A sad, ill man, close to death, but still David Golder! In London, Paris, New York, when someone said the name 'David Golder' it evoked an old, hardened Jew, who all his life had been hated and feared, who had crushed anyone who wanted to do him harm. 'The snakes . . .' he muttered, 'the snakes. Oh,

I'll teach them a lesson, before I die . . . since that's what she said: that I'm going to die. . .' His trembling hands were clutching the sheets; he looked at his heavy fingers, shaking with fever, with a sort of hopeless sadness. 'What have they done to me?' He closed his eyes, wincing in hatred. 'Gloria.' Her pearls had been as icy and slippery as a mass of slithering serpents . . . And as for the other one . . . that little whore . . . 'And what are they without me? Nothing, trash. I've worked, I've killed,' he said suddenly, out loud, in a strange voice; he stopped. 'Yes, I killed Simon Marcus,' he said, slowly wringing his hands, 'I know I did . . . Come on, you know very well, you did,' he muttered darkly to himself, 'and now . . . So they think I'm going to carry on working like a dog until I drop dead, well if that's what they think, they've got another think coming!' He let out a sharp, bizarre little laugh that sounded as if he were being strangled. 'That mad old hag . . . and as for the other one, the . . .' He swore in Yiddish, cursing her in a low voice. 'No, my pretty one, it's over, I'm telling you, all over . . .'

It was light now. He could hear someone at his door. 'What is it?' he called out mechanically.

'It's a telegram, Sir.'

'Come in.'

The servant entered. 'Are you ill, Sir?'

He didn't reply. He took the telegram and opened it. 'NEED MONEY. JOYCE.'

'If you would like to reply, Sir,' the servant said, looking at him oddly, 'the messenger is still here . . .'

'What was that?' he said slowly. 'No . . . There's no reply.'

He got back into bed and lay there motionless, his eyes closed. That was how Loewe found him, a few hours later. He hadn't moved. He was breathing with great difficulty, his face contorted with pain, his head thrown back, his quivering lips colourless with fever and thirst.

He refused to get up, to speak; he uttered not a single

order, not a word; he seemed half dead, not of this world. Loewe put letters into his hands: letters with demands for money, delays, assistance, but he signed none of them; they just fell from his lifeless fingers. Loewe, terrified, left the same night.

Three days later, David Golder's crash on the Stock Market was over, dragging down many other fortunes along with his own, like a senseless tide.

Joyce and Alec planned to spend the night near Ascain. They had left Madrid ten days earlier and were wandering through the Pyrenees, unable to tear themselves from each other's arms.

Joyce usually drove, while Alec and her dog, Jill, dozed, worn out by the heat of the sun. They would stop when it was dark and have dinner in the garden of some rural hotel where couples in love were serenaded by accordion players. The wisteria was in full bloom, and the trees hung with paper lanterns that sometimes caught light in a burst of golden flame that lapped at the leaves before turning to ash and falling to the ground. The young couple would sit at a wobbly wooden table caressing each other, while a girl with her hair tied back in a dark headscarf served them chilled wine. Then they would go upstairs to spend the night in a sparsely furnished, cool bedroom, where they would make love, fall asleep, then leave the next day.

As evening fell, they were driving along a road near Ascain, in the mountains. The setting sun bathed the houses of the small village in a pale-pink light the colour of sugared almonds.

'Tomorrow,' said Alec, 'it's back to work . . . Lady Rovenna . . .'

'Oh!' muttered Joyce, angrily. 'She's so ghastly, so ugly and mean . . .'

'We have to live,' he said, then added, laughing, 'When

we're married, Joy, I'll only sleep with pretty young women.'
He placed a gentle hand on Joy's delicate neck and gave it
a squeeze. 'Joy, I really want you, you know that. Only
you . . .'

'Of course I know,' said Joy, glibly, her lovely painted lips
in a triumphant little pout, 'Of course I know.'

It was getting darker. Deep within the Pyrenees, the
peaceful little clouds that formed at night were beginning to
slip down into the valleys where they would nestle until
morning. Joyce stopped the car outside a hotel. A woman
came out and opened the car door. 'Monsieur, Madame. A
single room with a large bed?' she asked with a smile, as
soon as she saw them.

It was a very large room with a pale wood floor and an
enormous, high bed. Joyce ran and threw herself down on
the flowered quilt.

'Alec . . . come here . . .'

He leaned over her.

A little later, she gave a moan: 'Mosquitoes . . . look . . .'

They were flying around the light on the ceiling. Alec
quickly switched it off. Night had secretly, suddenly descended
while they were kissing. Through the window, from the
narrow garden full of sunflowers, came the sound of water
flowing in a fountain.

'Where's the white wine we left to chill?' asked Alec, his
eyes shining. 'I'm hungry and thirsty . . .'

'What have we got to eat?'

'I ordered some crayfish and the wine,' said Alec. 'As for
the rest, we'll have to make do with the dish of the day, my
love. Do you realise we only have five hundred francs left?
We've spent fifty thousand in ten days. If your father doesn't
send you some money . . .'

'When I think of that man,' said Joyce, bitterly, 'how he
let me leave without a penny! I'll never forgive him. If it
hadn't been for old Fischl . . .'

'What exactly did old Fischl ask you to do for his fifty thousand francs?' asked Alec, coyly.

'Nothing!' she shouted crossly, 'I swear! Just the idea of him touching me with his ugly hands is enough to make me sick! You're the one who sleeps with old women like Lady Rovenna for money, you horrible little toad!'

She covered his mouth with hers and angrily bit his lip as if it were a piece of fruit.

Alec let out a cry. 'Oh! I'm bleeding, you horrible little beast, look . . .'

She laughed in the darkness.

'Come on, let's go downstairs . . .'

They went out into the garden, Jill following close behind them. They were alone; the hotel seemed empty. In the clear evening sky, a large yellow moon hung suspended between the trees. Joy lifted the lid of the steaming hot soup tureen, breathing in its aroma with a little purr of pleasure.

'Oh, that smells good . . . Give me your bowl . . .'

She served him standing up; she looked so strange with her make-up, her bare arms and her pearls flung behind her that he suddenly burst out laughing as he watched her.

'What's the matter?'

'Oh, nothing . . . It's funny . . . You don't look like a woman who . . .'

'A *young* woman,' she interrupted, frowning.

'I can't picture you ever being a little girl . . . I bet you came into this world singing and dancing, with rings on your fingers and make-up on your eyes, didn't you? Do you know how to cut this bread? I want some.'

'No, do you?'

'No.'

They called the serving girl who cut the round, golden loaf, pressing it against her chest. Joy watched her, lazily stretching out her bare arms, with her head thrown back.

107

'When I was little, I was very beautiful . . . They would stroke me, tease me . . .'

'Who do you mean by *they*?'

'Men. Especially old men, of course . . .'

The servant took away the empty dishes and came back with an earthenware bowl of crayfish swimming in a steaming, delicious-smelling, spicy broth. They devoured them with great gusto. Joyce added even more pepper and then stuck out her tongue as if it were on fire. Alec slowly poured the chilled wine; it made the glasses turn misty.

'We'll have champagne in our room tonight, as we always do,' murmured Joyce, slightly tipsy, while cracking an enormous crayfish between her teeth. 'What kind of champagne do they have? I want some Cliquot, very dry.'

She raised her glass between her cupped hands.

'Look . . . the wine is the same colour as the moon tonight, all golden . . .'

They drank together from the same glass, merging their moist, peppery lips, lips so young that nothing could change the way they tasted of ripe fruit.

With the chicken sautéed with olives and sweet pimentos, they drank a bottle of ruby Chambertin, full-bodied and warm, that left a wonderful taste in the mouth. Then Alec ordered some brandy and poured drops of it into two large glasses of champagne. Joyce drank. While they were having dessert, she started acting wild. With her dog on her lap, she threw back her head, looked up at the sky, then, with all her strength, pulled the golden locks of her short hair straight into the air.

'I want to sleep outdoors all night . . . I want to spend my whole life here . . . I want to spend my whole life making love . . . What do you say?'

'I love your little breasts,' said Alec. Then he fell silent.

He didn't speak much when he drank. He continued pouring the brandy into the golden champagne, drop by drop.

It was a peaceful night in the country; the mountains were bathed in moonlight; the cicadas were chirping.

'They think it's daytime,' murmured Joyce, delighted. The little dog had fallen asleep in her arms; she didn't want to move. 'Alec,' she said, 'put a cigarette in my mouth and light it for me.'

Alec groped about in the dark, found a cigarette and put it between her lips, then passionately grabbed the back of her neck and muttered something she couldn't understand.

When Joy suddenly uncrossed her legs, the little dog woke up, jumped down, stretched out on the grass and nuzzled the moist, sweet-smelling September earth.

'Come, Joy,' Alec urged quietly, 'Come and play at love . . .'

'Come on, Jill,' Joyce said to her dog.

Jill looked up and seemed to hesitate. But the couple were already disappearing into the darkness, walking towards the house with slow, tottering steps, their young, intoxicated faces leaning towards one another. Jill got up with a throaty little noise that sounded like someone sighing and followed them, stopping every few steps to sniff the ground.

As usual, once inside the bedroom, the dog lay down facing the bed, and Joy repeated, as she did every night, 'Jill, you naughty girl, we should make you pay to watch!'

The moon spread great puddles of silver over the floor. Joy undressed slowly, then went and stood naked in front of the window, wearing only her pearls; they shimmered in the cool moonlight.

'I'm beautiful, aren't I Alec? Do you want me?'

'It's our last night together,' Alec replied wistfully, like a child. 'We have no more money, there's nothing left. We have to go back, we have to part . . . Until when?'

'My God, you're right . . .'

That night, for the first time, they didn't throw themselves hungrily into making love only to fall asleep afterwards, like wild young animals tired after doing battle; instead, with heavy hearts, they lay beneath the flower-covered quilt and, bathed in moonlight, cradled each other for a long time, wrapped in each other's arms, without speaking and almost without desire.

Then they felt cold, and closed the shutters, pulling the heavy blue and pink curtains across the window. The electricity had been turned off, it was late; a burning candle on the edge of the table sent their shadows dancing to the ceiling. They could hear, very far away, the muffled sound of hooves hitting the ground.

'There's a farm nearby, most likely,' said Alec, as Joy looked up. 'The animals must be dreaming . . .'

Jill, still asleep, turned over with a great sigh, so weary and sad that Joy laughed and whispered, 'Daddy sighs like that when he's lost on the Stock Market . . . Oh, Alec, your knees are so cold . . .'

On the white ceiling, their shadows mingled, forming an eerie knot, like a bouquet of flowers whose stems are entwined.

Joyce let her hands slide, slowly, down her trembling aching hips.

'Oh, Alec! I'm so in love with love . . .'

Golder returned to Paris alone. After the house in Biarritz had been sold, Gloria and Joyce went on a cruise on Behring's yacht, with Hoyos, Alec and the Mannerings. It was not until December that Gloria returned to Paris; she immediately came round with an antiques dealer to arrange the sale of the furniture.

It was with a kind of sardonic pleasure that Golder watched the contents of the apartment being taken away: the table decorated with bronze Sphinxes, the four-poster Louis XV bed, with its cupids, bows and arrows. For a long while now, he'd been sleeping in the sitting room, on a narrow, hard fold-out bed. Towards evening, when the final removal vans had gone, there remained nothing in the apartment except a few wicker chairs and a pine kitchen table. Wood shavings and old newspapers were scattered on the floor. Gloria came back. Golder hadn't moved. He was propped up on the bed, a black plaid blanket over his chest, looking with an expression of relief at the enormous bare windows, stripped of the damask curtains that had kept out the light and air.

The bare wood floor made Gloria's heavy footsteps sound even louder. The noise seemed to surprise her; she shuddered nervously, stopped, then started walking again on tiptoe, trying to keep her balance, but the noise didn't stop. She sat down opposite Golder.

'David . . .'

111

They looked at each other in silence for a moment, their eyes hard. She was trying to smile, but, despite her efforts, her harsh, square jaw jutted forward with a voracious movement that made her face look carnivorous when she wasn't careful.

'Well,' she said finally, nervously flicking the gloves she was holding, 'are you satisfied, are you happy now?'

'Yes,' he replied.

She clenched her teeth. 'You're mad . . .' she hissed quietly. 'You're a mad old fool . . .' Her voice was strange and sharp. 'So you think I'm going to starve to death without you and your damned money, do you? Well, just look at me . . . I don't exactly look very poor, do I? Have you seen this?' She shook her wrist at him, making her new bracelet jingle. 'Did you pay for that? No! So, what was this all about? What were you hoping to accomplish? You're the only one who's suffering, you fool . . . As for me, well, I'm managing . . . And everything that was here belongs to me, to me,' she repeated, angrily striking the wooden chair, 'and if you ever try to stop me from selling anything, however and whenever I want, you'll have me to deal with me, you thief! You should be thrown into prison,' she spat. 'To leave your wife penniless after so many years of marriage . . . Answer me, say something,' she shouted suddenly. 'You know very well that I can see the truth! Well? Admit it! You did it so I'd have no money . . . You've bankrupted yourself and so many other poor souls just for that. You'd rather die between these four walls just to see me poor as well, is that it? Well? Is it?'

'I don't give a damn about you,' said Golder. He closed his eyes. 'I really don't give a damn about you, if you only knew . . .' he murmured, 'not about you, your money or anything to do with you . . . And don't think your money will last, my poor girl. Believe me, when you have no husband to keep topping up the cash, it goes very quickly . . .' There was no anger in his voice. He spoke in the low, measured tones of an old man, pulling up the collar of his jacket against the cold. An icy wind blew in from the street through the cracks in the bare window. 'Yes, how quickly it goes . . . You've been playing the Stock Market, haven't you? They say that any stock you touch will go sky-high this year. But that won't last for ever . . . And as for Hoyos . . .' He let out a surprising little laugh that made him sound almost young. 'Oh, what a life you'll have in a year or two, you poor things!'

'And what about you? What about your life? You've buried yourself alive!'

'It's what I wanted to do,' Golder said abruptly with a kind of haughty anger, 'and I have always done what I wanted to do on this earth.'

She fell silent, and, very slowly, smoothed out her gloves.

'Are you going to stay here?'

'I don't know.'

'So you have some money left, then?' she murmured. 'You made sure you're all right . . .'

He nodded. 'Yes,' he said quietly, 'but don't try to get any of it. Save yourself the trouble. I've made very sure . . .'

She gave a scornful laugh, nodding at the empty room.

'Oh! I'm happy to be rid of all of that,' he said wearily, closing his eyes. 'The Sphinxes, the laurels . . . I don't need any of it.'

Picking up her fox stole and her handbag, Gloria went and stood in front of the mirror above the fireplace. She began carefully to powder her face.

'I think Joyce will be coming to see you soon . . .'

When he didn't respond, she murmured, 'She needs money . . .'

In the mirror, she could see a strange look pass over Golder's hard face.

'All this is because of Joyce,' she said quietly and quickly, almost in spite of herself, 'isn't it?'

113

She could clearly see his cheeks and hands quivering, as if overcome by a sudden chill.

'It's all because of Joyce. And yet Joyce hasn't done anything to you . . . How ironic.'

She let out a forced laugh, dry and bitter.

'You adore her . . . My God, you adore her . . . just like an old lover . . . It's grotesque . . .'

'That's enough,' shouted Golder.

Her instinct was to recoil in fear, but she restrained herself.

'So,' she whispered, raising her eyebrows, 'are you starting at that again? Do you want me to have you locked up?'

'I wouldn't put it past you . . .' he sighed, sounding angry and tired. 'Get out.'

He seemed to be making a great effort to stay calm. Very slowly, he wiped away the sweat that was running down his face.

'Go. I'm asking you to go.'

'Well, then, I suppose this is goodbye?'

Without replying, he stood up and went into the next room. The thud of the door closing behind him echoed through the empty house. She remembered that he had always ended their quarrels like this. Then she realised that she would probably never see him again. This solitary life would undoubtedly finish him off, and soon . . . 'To have lived so many years together to end up like this . . . And why? At their age . . . Over things that happen all the time . . . He made it happen . . . Well, it was his loss . . . But how ridiculous it was, by God . . . how ridiculous . . .'

She closed the door of the apartment and walked wearily down the stairs.

Golder was alone.

Golder was on his own for a long time. At least his family wasn't bothering him any more.

The doctor came to see him every morning; quickly walking through the dark rooms, he would go into Golder's bedroom, place a stethoscope on his old chest and listen to the results of the night's heavy, laboured breathing. But Golder's heart condition was improving. The pain had subsided. And Golder, too, seemed to have subsided into a kind of slumber, a depressed stupor. He would get up and dress, trying to move as slowly as possible in order to save as much strength, as much of his life force as he could. Then he would walk around the apartment twice, aware of every movement of his muscles, every beat of his pulse and heart. After that, he would measure out his medicine himself, one gram at a time, on the kitchen scales, then boil an egg using his watch as a timer.

In the enormous kitchen, spacious enough for five servants in the past, there was now just one elderly maid, hunched over the stove, who prepared his meals. She watched with weary resignation as he paced back and forth, his hands clasped behind his back, in a dressing gown he'd bought years before in London; its purple silk was so faded and torn that tufts of the white wool lining were sticking through the fabric.

Breakfast over, he would have an armchair and footstool

115

placed by the sitting-room window, and he would sit there all day long, playing Solitaire on a tray on his lap. If it was sunny, he would visit the chemist's in the next street, weigh himself, and walk slowly back home, leaning heavily on his walking stick and stopping every fifty paces to catch his breath, his left hand carefully holding closed the ends of his woollen scarf that was wrapped twice around his neck and fastened with a pin.

Then, when night began to fall, Soifer would come round to play cards. He was an old German Jew Golder had known in Silesia; they'd lost touch but then run into each other a few months earlier. Bankrupted by inflation, Soifer had played the money markets and won everything back again. In spite of that, he had retained a mistrust of money, and the way revolutions and wars could transform it overnight into nothing but worthless bits of paper. It was a mistrust that seemed to grow as the years passed, and little by little, Soifer had invested his fortune in jewellery. He kept everything in a safe in London: diamonds, pearls, emeralds – all so beautiful that even Gloria had never owned any that could compare. Despite all this, his meannesss bordered on madness. He lived in a sordid little furnished room, in a dingy street near Passy, and would never take taxis, even when a friend offered to pay. 'I do not wish,' he would say, 'to indulge in luxuries that I can't afford myself.' Instead, he would wait for the bus in the rain, in winter, for hours at a time, letting them go by one after the other if there was no room left in second class. All his life, he had walked on tiptoe so his shoes would last longer. For several years now, since he had lost all his teeth, he only ate cereal and puréed vegetables to avoid having to buy dentures.

His yellow skin, as dry and transparent as an autumn leaf, gave him a look of pathetic nobility, the same kind of look that old criminals sometimes have. His head was crowned with beautiful tufts of silvery white hair. It was only his gaping, spluttering mouth, buried in the deep ridges of his face, that inspired a feeling of revulsion and fear.

Every day, Golder would let him win twenty francs or so, and listen to him talk about other people's business deals. Soifer possessed a kind of dark sense of humour that was very similar to Golder's and meant that they got along together well.

Much later, Soifer would die all alone, like a dog, without a friend, without a single wreath on his grave, buried in the cheapest cemetery in Paris by his family, who hated him, and whom he had hated, but to whom he nevertheless left a fortune of some thirty million francs, thus fulfilling till the end the incomprehensible destiny of every good Jew on this earth.

And so, at five o'clock every day, sitting at a pine table in front of the sitting-room window, Golder wearing his purple dressing gown, Soifer with a woman's black wool shawl draped over his shoulders, the two men played cards. In the silent apartment, Golder's coughing fits echoed with a strange, hollow sound. Old Soifer moaned about his life in an annoyed, plaintive tone of voice.

Beside them, hot tea sat in two large, silver-bottomed glasses, part of a set that Golder, long ago, had ordered from Russia. Soifer would put his cards down on the table, automatically shielding them with his hand, take a sip of tea and say, 'You know that sugar is going to go up again?' Then: 'You know that the Banque Lalleman is going to finance the Franco-Algerian Mining Company?' And Golder would look up abruptly with an eager, lively expression, like a flame that flickers up from the ashes and then dies down again.

'That should be a pretty good deal,' he replied wearily.

'The only good deal is to invest your money in something safe – if there is such a thing – then sit on it and protect it like an old hen. Your turn, Golder . . .'

They went back to playing cards.

'Have you heard?' said Soifer as he came in, 'Have you heard what they've cooked up now?'

'Who?'

Soifer shook his fist at the window, indicating all of Paris.

'First it was income tax,' he continued in a shrill, quivering voice, 'soon there will be a tax on rent. Last week I spent forty-three francs on heating. Then my wife went and bought a new hat. Seventy-two francs! And it looks like a pot that's been turned upside down! I don't mind paying for something of quality, something that lasts, but that hat . . . It won't even last her two seasons. And at her age! What she could do with is a shroud! I would have paid for that with pleasure . . . Seventy-two francs! In my day, where we lived, we could buy a bearskin coat for that price. My God, if my son ever says he wants to get married, I'll strangle him with my bare hands. He'd be better off dead, the poor boy, than to have to keep paying for things his whole life, like you and me. And I heard just today that if I don't renew my identity card right away, I'll be deported. A miserable, sickly old man! I ask you, where would I go?'

'To Germany?'

'Oh, sure, to Germany,' Soifer grumbled. 'Germany can go to hell! You know what happened to me before in Germany, when I had that trouble over providing them with war supplies. No? You didn't know? Look, I've got to get going now, their

118

office closes at four o'clock ... And do you know how much it will cost me, for the pleasure? Three hundred francs, my dear Golder, three hundred francs plus their administrative costs, not to mention the time wasted and the twenty francs you always let me win, since we won't have time to play cards today. Oh, dear Lord! Why don't you come along with me? It will take your mind off things, it's nice out.'

'Do you want me to come so I can pay for the taxi?' asked Golder with a smile that twisted his face like a sudden fit of coughing.

'Good heavens,' said Soifer, 'I was expecting to take the tram ... And you know I never take taxis in order to avoid getting into bad habits ... But today, my old legs feel as heavy as lead ... And as long as *you* don't mind throwing your money out of the window?'

They went out together, each of them leaning on a walking stick. Golder listened quietly as his friend explained how a recent sugar deal had just ended in bankruptcy because of some sort of fraud. Soifer rubbed his trembling hands together in an expression of sheer delight as he reeled off figures and the names of the ruined shareholders,

When they left the Police station, Golder felt like walking. It was still light; the final rays of the red winter sun lit up the Seine. They crossed the bridge, strolled up a street they chanced upon behind the Hôtel de Ville, then along another street that turned out to be the Rue Vieille-du-Temple.

Suddenly, Soifer stopped.

'Do you know where we are?'

'No,' replied Golder, indifferent.

'Right over there, my friend, on the Rue des Rosiers, there's a little Jewish restaurant, the only one in Paris where they know how to make a good stuffed pike. Come and have dinner with me.'

'You don't think I'm going to eat stuffed pike,' Golder grumbled, 'when I haven't touched fish or meat in six months?'

'No one's asking you to eat anything. Just come and pay. All right?'

'Go to hell.'

Nevertheless, he followed Soifer who was limping painfully down the street, breathing in the smell of fish, dust and rotting straw. Soifer turned round and put his arm through Golder's.

'A dirty Jewish neighbourhood, isn't it?' he said affectionately. 'Does it remind you of anything?'

'Nothing good,' Golder replied darkly.

He stopped and, for a moment, looked up at the houses, laundry hanging from their windows, without speaking. Some children rushed past his legs. He gently pushed them away with his cane and sighed. In the shops, there was hardly anything to buy except second-hand clothes or herring in tubs of brine. Soifer pointed to a small restaurant with a sign written in Hebrew.

'Here it is. Are you coming Golder? You're happy to buy me dinner, aren't you? To make a poor old man happy?'

'Oh, go to hell!' repeated Golder. But he continued to follow Soifer. What difference did it make where he went? He felt more tired than usual.

The little restaurant seemed quite clean. It had brightly coloured paper tablecloths and a shiny brass kettle in one corner of the room. Not a soul in sight.

Soifer ordered a portion of stuffed pike and some horseradish. With great reverence, he picked up the hot plate and lifted it to his nose. 'It smells so good!'

'Oh, for goodness sake, just eat and leave me in peace,' murmured Golder.

He turned round and lifted a corner of the heavy red and white checked curtain. Outside, two men had stopped and were leaning against the window, talking. He couldn't hear what they were saying, but Golder could understand by the way they gestured with their hands. One of them was Polish

120

and wore an extraordinary, dilapidated fur hat with earflaps; he had an enormous curly, grey beard that he impatiently stroked, plaited, twirled and untwisted endlessly, at great speed. The other one was a young boy with red hair that burst out in all directions, like flames.

'I wonder what they sell,' thought Golder. 'Hay and scrap iron, like in my day?'

He half closed his eyes. Now, as night began to fall, the tops of the houses were cloaked in shadow, and the clatter and creak of a handcart drowned out the sound of the cars on the Rue Vieille-du-Temple, he felt as if he had been transported back in time to the old country, was seeing once again those familiar faces, but distorted, deformed, as in a dream . . .

'There are dreams like this,' he thought vaguely, 'where you see people who have died years before . . .'

'What are you looking at?' asked Soifer. He pushed away his plate, which still contained the remains of some fish and bits of mashed potato. 'Ah, so this is what it's like to grow old . . . In the past, I would have happily eaten three portions like this! But now, my poor teeth . . . I have to swallow without chewing. It gives me heartburn here . . .' He pointed to his chest. 'What are you thinking about?'

He stopped, watched Golder and shook his head.

'Oy,' he said suddenly, in his inimitable tone of voice that was plaintive and ironic at the same time, 'Oy, Lord God! They're happier than we are, don't you think? Dirty and poor, all right, but does a Jew need much? Poverty preserves the Jews like brine preserves the herrings. I'd like to come here more often. If it weren't so far, and especially, so expensive – it's expensive everywhere nowadays – I'd come here every night to have a peaceful meal, without my family, who can all go to hell . . .'

'We should come here now and again,' murmured Golder.

He stretched out his hands towards the glowing stove that

had just been lit; it radiated a heavy smell of heat from its corner.

'At home,' he thought, 'a smell like that would make me choke . . .'

But he didn't feel sick. A kind of sensual warmth, something he'd never felt before, seeped deep into his old bones.

Outside, a man walked by carrying a long pole; he touched the street lamp opposite the restaurant and a flame shot out, lighting up a narrow, dark window where washing was hanging above some empty old flowerpots. Golder suddenly remembered a little crooked window just like it, opposite the shop where he'd been born . . . remembered his street, in the wind and snow, as it sometimes appeared in his dreams.

'It's a long road,' he said out loud.

'Yes,' said Soifer, 'long, hard and pointless.'

Both of them looked up, and for a long while gazed, sighing, at the miserable window, the worn-out clothes beating against the panes of glass. A woman opened the window and leaned out to pull in the washing. She shook it out, then bent forward, took a little mirror out of her pocket and used the light from the street lamp to put on some lipstick.

Golder suddenly stood up.

'Let's go home . . . the smell from that oil stove is making me feel sick . . .'

That night he dreamt of Joyce, her features mingling with those of the little Jewish woman he'd seen on the Rue des Rosiers. It was the first time in a long while. The memory of Joy lay dormant within him, like his pain . . .

He woke up, his legs shaking and as tired as if he had walked for miles. All day long he sat wrapped in blankets and shawls looking out of the window; his cards lay untouched. He was shivering; an insidious, icy chill seemed to pierce him, right down to his bones.

Soifer arrived later that evening, but he too felt unwell and melancholy and hardly spoke. He left earlier than usual, hurrying down the dark street, his umbrella clutched to his chest.

Golder ate dinner. Then, when the maid had gone up to bed, he walked around the apartment, locking all the doors. Gloria had had all the chandeliers taken away. In every room, an electric bulb hung from a long wire; they swayed in the draught and lit up Golder's reflection in the mirrors above the fireplaces. There he was, barefoot, holding his keys, with his wild, thick white hair and strikingly pale face, each day showing more and more of that bluish tint common amongst people with a heart condition.

The doorbell rang. Before answering it, Golder looked in surprise at the time. The evening papers had arrived long ago. Perhaps Soifer had had an accident . . .

'Is that you, Soifer?' he asked through the door. 'Who is it?'

'Tübingen,' a voice replied.

123

Golder, his face suddenly overwhelmed with emotion, unfastened the security chain. His hands were unsteady and he grew impatient with himself as he fumbled about, but Tübingen waited without saying a word. Golder knew that he could remain like that, motionless, for hours on end. 'He hasn't changed a bit,' he thought.

Finally, he managed to unlock the door. Tübingen came in. 'Hello,' he said.

He took off his hat and coat, hanging them up himself, then opened his wet umbrella, set it in the corner and shook Golder's hand.

His long head was oddly shaped, in such a way that his forehead looked too big and luminous. He had a puritanical, pale face, with thin lips.

'May I come in?' he asked, pointing to the sitting room.

'Yes, please do . . .'

Golder saw him glance around the bare rooms and lower his eyes, like someone who has intruded on a secret.

'My wife has left,' he said.

'Biarritz?'

'I don't know.'

'Ah,' murmured Tübingen.

He sat down; Golder sat opposite him, breathing with difficulty.

'How's business?' he asked finally.

'The same as ever. Some good, some bad. You know that Amrum signed with the Russians?'

'What? For the Teisk shares?' Golder quickly asked, leaning forward suddenly as if he wanted to grasp a fleeting shadow. Then he let his hands drop back down and shrugged his shoulders. 'I didn't know,' he said, sighing.

'Not for the Teisk's shares. The contract stipulates the sale of a hundred thousand tons of Russian oil per year for five years, in Constantinople, Port-Said and Colombo.

'But . . . what about Teisk?' Golder muttered.

124

'Not mentioned.'

'Ah.'

'I knew that Amrum had sent agents to Moscow twice, but nothing came of it.'

'Why?'

'Why? Perhaps because the Soviets wanted to get a loan of twenty-three million gold roubles from the United States and Amrum had to pay off three members of the government, including a Senator. It was all too much. And they also made the mistake of letting the evidence get stolen, which blew up in the press.

'Oh, really?'

'Yes.'

He nodded. 'Amrum have paid dearly for our Persian oil fields, Golder.'

'You've started up negotiations again?'

'Of course. Straight away. I wanted to own the whole of the Caucasus region. I wanted a monopoly on oil refinery and to become the sole distributor of Russian petroleum products in the world.'

Golder smirked.

'You wanted too much, as you yourself just pointed out. They don't like giving foreigners such economic influence and consequently too much political power.'

'The fools. I'm not interested in their politics. People can do what they want in their own country. Once I was there, they wouldn't have had their noses stuck into my business affairs, I can promise you that.'

'If it had been me . . .' Golder began musing out loud, 'I would have started with Teisk and the Aroundgis. Then gradually, after a while,' he opened his hand and quickly closed it, 'I would have snapped it all up. All of it. All of the Caucasus, all the oil . . .'

'That's why I've come to see you; I want you to handle the deal.'

DAVID GOLDER

Golder shrugged his shoulders.

'No. I'm out of it now. I'm ill . . . half dead.'

'Did you keep your Teisk shares?'

'Yes,' said Golder, hesitating, 'I don't know why . . . They were hardly worth anything. I could sell them as scrap paper . . .'

'That's true enough, but only if Amrum wins the concession. Then I'll be damned if they're worth even that. But if *I* win . . .'

He fell silent. Golder shook his head.

'No,' he said, clenching his teeth, a look of suffering on his face. 'No.'

'Why not? I need you. And you need me.'

'I know. But I don't want to work anymore. I can't. I'm not well. My heart . . . I know that if I don't give up work entirely, and right away, I'm a dead man. I'm not interested. What for? I don't need much now, at my age. I just need to stay alive.'

Tübingen shook his head.

'I'm seventy-two years old,' he said. 'In twenty or twenty-five years' time, when all the Teisk oil wells start producing, I'll have been dead a very long time. I think about that sometimes . . . when I'm signing a ninety-nine-year lease! By then, it won't just be me, but my son and my grandsons and their children who will all be in the hands of the Lord. But there will always be a Tübingen. And that's why I keep going.'

'But I don't have anyone,' said Golder, 'so, what's the use?'

'You have children, like I do.'

'I have no one,' Golder repeated, angrily.

Tübingen closed his eyes. 'There would still be something that you'd created.'

He slowly opened his eyes and appeared to look straight through Golder.

126

'Something,' he repeated eagerly in the deep voice of a man who is revealing the secret thing most dear to his heart, 'something that you'd built, that was lasting . . .'

'And what is it that's lasting for me? Money? Oh, it's not worth the trouble . . . unless you could take it with you . . .'

'*The Lord giveth and the Lord taketh away. Blessed be the name of the Lord*,' Tübingen recited quietly, with the droning intonation of a puritan brought up on the Scriptures since childhood. 'That's the law. There's nothing you can do.'

Golder sighed deeply.

'No. Nothing.'

'It's me,' said Joyce. She came so close that she was nearly touching him, but he didn't move.

'Anyone would think you didn't recognise me.'

Then she cried out 'Dad!' as she had in the past.

It was only then that he shuddered and closed his eyes, as if blinded by a dazzling light. He stretched out his hand so weakly that it barely touched hers before it dropped down on to his knee; still he said nothing.

She pulled a footstool up to his armchair, sat down and took off her hat, vigorously shaking her head in the way that was so familiar to him . . . Then she waited, silently.

'You've changed,' he whispered, in spite of himself.

'Yes' she said with a bitter laugh.

She was taller and thinner, with an indefinable look of weariness, distress and resignation.

She was wearing a magnificent sable coat. She threw it down on to the floor behind her, revealing her neck and, in place of the pearls Golder had given her, an emerald necklace, as green as grass, its stones so pure and enormous that Golder stared at it for a moment, speechless with disbelief. Finally, he laughed harshly.

'Ah, yes, I see now . . . You've sorted yourself out too . . . So why have you come then? I don't understand . . .'

'It's a gift from my fiancé,' she said quietly, with no emotion. 'I have to get married soon.'

'Ah . . . Congratulations,' he added, with difficulty.

She didn't reply.

He thought for a moment, wiped his forehead several times, then sighed, 'Well then, I wish you . . .' He hesitated. 'So he's rich, is he? You should be happy. . .'

'Happy!' She let out a cry of despair and turned towards him. 'Happy? Do you know who I'm going to marry?'

He didn't answer.

'Old Fischl,' she shouted, 'that's who!'

'Fischl!'

'Yes, Fischl! What did you think I would do? I have no money now, do I? My mother gives me nothing, not a penny. You know her, she'd rather see me starve to death than give me any money, wouldn't she? So, what do you expect? It's lucky he wants to marry me . . . Otherwise I would have just had to sleep with him, wouldn't I? Although that might have been better, easier at least, one night with him from time to time . . . but that's not what he wants, you see? The horrible old pig wants to get his money's worth!' Her voice suddenly quivered with hatred. 'Oh, I'd like to . . .' She stopped, ran her fingers through her hair and pulled it with all her might with a look of despair.

'I'd like to kill him,' she said slowly.

Golder managed to laugh.

'But why? It's a very good idea, it's wonderful! Fischl . . . He's rich, you know, when he's not in prison, and you'll cheat on him with your young man . . . what was his name . . . your little gigolo? And you'll be very happy. Come on! This was how you were meant to end up, you little slut, it was written all over your face . . . Still . . . still, it's not what I used to dream of for you, Joyce . . .'

His face grew even paler. 'Why should it matter to me, dear Lord?' he thought frantically, 'Why should it matter to me? Let her sleep with whomever she likes, let her go wherever she pleases . . .'

But his proud heart was bleeding, as it had in the past.

My daughter . . . (in spite of everything, everyone thought she was Golder's daughter) and Fischl!

'I'm so unhappy, if you only knew . . .'

'You want too much, my girl. Money, love, you have to choose . . . But you've made your choice, haven't you?' He winced in pain. 'No one's forcing you, are they? So, why are you whining? It's what you want.'

'Oh, this is all your fault, all of it! It's all because of you! How am I supposed to live with no money? I've tried, I swear to you I've tried . . . If you could have seen me last winter . . . You remember how cold it was? Just like it always is, right? And there I was walking around in my little grey autumn coat . . . the last thing I bought for myself before you left. Wasn't I a pretty sight! But I can't, I just can't do it, I'm not cut out for it, I'm telling you! It's not my fault! Then I got into debt, had all sorts of financial troubles . . . So, to put an end to them, I did what I had to do, didn't I? If it hadn't been him, it would have been someone else. But Alec, Alec! You say I'll cheat on Fischl. Of course I will! But if you think he's going to make it easy for me, you're very wrong. Oh, you don't know him! Once he'd paid for something, he watches over it, you know, he doesn't let it out of his sight. He's a dirty . . . a dirty old man! Oh, I just want to die, I'm so miserable, I'm so alone. I'm suffering, Dad. Help me. You're all I have!'

She clasped his hands and wrung them in despair.

'Speak to me!' she shouted. 'Say something! Otherwise I'm going to walk out of here and kill myself. Remember Marcus? They say he killed himself because of you . . . Well, you'll have my death on your conscience too, do you hear me?'

Her shrill, childlike voice echoed eerily in the empty rooms. Golder clenched his teeth.

'So you think you can frighten me, do you? Don't think I'm a fool! And besides, I haven't got any more money. Just leave me alone. You mean nothing to me. You know very well . . . You've always known . . . You're not my daughter . . . You're . . . You're Hoyos's daughter and you know it! Well, go and see him. Let *him* protect you, let *him* look after you, let *him* work to support you. It's his turn now. As for me, well, I've done quite enough for you, you're no longer my problem. Go away, you mean nothing to me anymore. Just get out!'

'Hoyos? Are you sure? Oh, Dad! If you only knew! Alec and I meet at his place . . . and we . . . with him right there . . .' She hid her face in her hands. He could see tears running through her fingers.

'Dad, you're all I have! I have no one else in the world!' she repeated, in despair. 'I couldn't care less that you're not my father, you have to believe me . . . You're all I have! Help me, I'm begging you. I want so much to be happy. I'm young, I want to live, I want . . . I want to be happy!'

'You're not the only one, my poor darling . . . Leave me now, leave me . . .'

He made a vague gesture with his hand that simultaneously pushed her away and drew her closer. Then he gave a sudden shudder and allowed his fingers to stroke her neck, her bowed head, her short, golden, sweet-smelling hair . . . Oh, he had missed touching her so much, missed feeling beneath his hand that blossoming, urgent spark of life, as in the past . . . and . . .

'Oh, Joyce!' he whispered, his heart breaking. 'Why did you come, Joyce? I was at peace . . .'

'My God, where else could I go?' She was nervously wringing her hands. 'Oh, if you would . . . if only you would . . .'

Golder shrugged his shoulders. 'What? You want me to give you Alec for life, buy him for you, like I used to buy you toys and jewellery? Is that it? But I can't do it now. It's too expensive. Did your mother tell you I still had money?'

'Yes.'

'Look at how I live. I barely have enough to see me through until I die. But it would only last *you* a year.'

'But why don't you do what you did before?' she begged desperately. 'Get back into business, make money? It's so easy . . .'

'Really! Is that what you think?'

Once again, with a kind of fearful tenderness, he touched her fine golden hair. 'Poor little Joyce . . .'

'It's funny,' he thought, painfully, 'I know exactly what will happen. In two months' time, she'll have had enough of sleeping with her Alec. . . or whoever else it is . . . and that will be that . . . But Fischl! Oh, if it were only someone else . . . anyone else! But Fischl!' He was filled with hatred. 'The bastard would talk about "Golder's daughter, whom I married even though she had nothing . . . nothing but the clothes on her back!"'

He leaned forward abruptly, took Joyce's face in both hands and raised it up, digging his old, hard nails into her delicate skin with a kind of urgency. 'You . . . you . . . If you didn't need me, you'd have left me here to die all alone, wouldn't you? Well, wouldn't you?'

'Would you have sent for me?' she whispered.

She smiled. He looked helplessly at her tear-filled eyes and her beautiful, full red lips that opened slowly, like a flower.

'My little girl,' he thought. 'Perhaps, after all, she *is* mine, who knows? And anyway, what does it matter, for God's sake, what difference does it make?'

'You really know how to get what you want from your old man, eh, Joy?' he whispered passionately. 'Your tears . . . and the idea of that pig being able to buy something that was mine, right? Right?' he repeated wildly, with a mixture of hatred and savage tenderness. 'So then, you want me to try? You want me to make you some more money before I die? Are you prepared to wait a year? A year from now, you'll be richer than your mother ever was.'

He let her go and stood up. He could feel the heat and energy of life coursing through his old, weary body once more – all the strength and passion he had felt in the past.

'Tell Fischl he can go to hell,' he continued. His voice had become precise, matter-of-fact. 'And if you weren't a complete fool, you'd send your Alec packing as well. No? If you let him spend all your money, what will you do after I'm gone? You don't care, is that it? You think you'll always be able to fall back on Fischl? Oh, I'm nothing but an old fool,' he growled. He took Joyce by the chin, gripping it so tightly that she winced in pain. 'You will do me the honour of signing the marriage contract I will have drawn up for you, and no questions asked. I'm not going to kill myself for your little gigolo. Understood? Do you want some money now?'

She nodded without replying. He let go of her, opened a drawer.

'Listen to me, Joy . . . Tomorrow you will go and see Seton, my lawyer. I'll instruct him to send you a hundred and fifty pounds every month . . .'

He quickly scribbled some figures in the margin of a newspaper that was laying on the table.

'That's just about what I used to give you. A bit less. But you'll have to make do with it for a while longer, my child, because it's all that I have left. Later on, after I get back, you can get married.'

'But where are you going?'

He shrugged his shoulders angrily.

'Do you really care?'

He put his hand on her neck. 'Joyce . . . If I die while I'm away, Seton will take care of everything to protect your interests. All you have to do is listen to him. Sign whatever he tells you to sign. Do you understand?'

She nodded.

He took a deep breath. 'So . . . that's it then . . .'

'Daddy, darling . . .'

She had slipped on to his lap, buried her head in his shoulder, closed her eyes.

He looked at her with a faint smile – a mere quiver of the lips that he quickly repressed. 'How loving people are when they're poor, eh? This is the first time I've seen you like this, my child . . .'

And the last . . . he thought, but he said nothing. He was happy simply to stroke her eyelids and neck. He did so for a long while, as if he were sculpting her features so he could remember them for a very long time to come.

'Both Parties agree to conclude the Agreement regarding concessions within thirty days of the signature of this Contract . . .'

The ten men sitting around the table all looked at Golder. 'Yes, go on,' he murmured.

'. . . in accordance with the following conditions . . .'

Golder fanned his face nervously with his hand in an attempt to dispel the cloud of smoke that threatened to choke him. The room was so thick with it that, from time to time, he could barely see the man opposite him who was reading: his pale, angular face and his black hole of a mouth became a mere patch of colour in the fog.

A strong odour of leather, sweat and Russian tobacco hung in the air.

Since the night before, these ten men had not managed to agree on the final wording of the contract. And before that, their negotiations had lasted eighteen weeks.

He glanced at his wrist to check the time, but his watch had stopped. He looked over at the window. Through the dirty glass, he could see the sun rising over Moscow. It was a very beautiful August morning, yet already it held the icy, transparent purity of the first dawns of autumn.

'The Soviet Government shall grant the Tübingen Petroleum Company a concession of up to fifty per cent of the oil fields located between the Teisk region and the area known as the Aroundgis, as described in the memorandum presented by the Tübingen Petroleum Company's representative, dated 2 December 1925. Each oil field included in this concession shall be rectangular in shape, no larger than one hundred acres, and shall not be adjoining . . .'

Golder interrupted.

'Would you please re-read that last item again for me?' he asked, his lips closing tightly.

'Each oil field . . .'

'So there it is,' thought Golder in frustration. 'No mention of that before . . . They wait until the very last minute to sneak in their dirty little ambiguous clauses that don't seem to mean anything precise, just to have an excuse to break the agreement later on, after we've advanced them the money for the initial expenses. I heard they did the same thing to Amrum . . .'

He remembered having read a copy of the Amrum contract, the one he'd found amongst Marcus's papers. Work was supposed to begin on a certain date. They had unofficially promised Amrum's representative that the date could be extended – then they claimed the contract had been broken. It had cost Amrum millions. 'Bunch of pigs,' he muttered.

He banged his fist down on the table angrily.

'You will cross that out right now!'

'No,' someone shouted.

'Then I'm not signing.'

'Oh, but my dear David Issakitch . . .' one of the men cried.

His warm, lyrical Russian accent and his soothing, considerate Slavonic expression jarred strangely with the severe, narrow eyes set in his yellow face, and their intent, cruel stare.

'What do you mean, my dear friend?' he said, stretching out his arms as if he wanted to hug Golder. 'Goloubtchik . . . you know very well that this clause doesn't mean anything significant. It is only there to appease the legitimate concerns of the Proletariat who would not look favourably on having a part of Soviet territory pass into the hands of Capitalists without some assurances . . .'

Golder brushed him away.

'Enough! What next! And what about Amrum, eh? In any case, I am not entitled to sign any clause that has not been read and approved by the company. Have I made myself clear, Simon Alexeevitch?'

Simon Alexeevitch closed his file. 'Perfectly clear,' he said, in a different tone of voice. 'We'll wait then so the company has time to consider it and either accept or reject it.'

'So that's it . . .' thought Golder. 'They want to drag it out some more . . . Perhaps Amrum . . .'

He flung his chair aside and stood up. 'There will be no more delays, do you understand? No more delays! This contract will be signed right now or not at all! You'd better be careful! It's yes or no, but right now! I refuse to spend even one extra hour in Moscow, let there be no misunderstandings! Come on, Valleys,' he said, turning towards the secretary of the Tübingen Company, who hadn't slept in thirty-six hours and was looking at him in a kind of despair. Were they going to have to start all over again, my God, over something so insignificant? These endless negotiations, the shouting, Golder with his strangled, terrifying voice that at times seemed like nothing more than a kind of inarticulate babbling, like the sound of blood catching in your throat . . .

'How can he shout like that?' thought Valleys with an instinctive feeling of terror, 'and the rest of them as well?'

They were now all huddled together at one end of the room, shouting wildly. Valleys could only make out certain words – 'the interests of the Proletariat', 'the tyranny and exploitation of the Capitalists' – which they hurled at each other in rapid fire as if they were punching each other in the face.

Golder, red with fury, was frantically hammering the table with his hand, sending papers flying in all directions. Every time he shouted, Valleys thought the old man's heart would explode.

'Valleys! For God's sake!'

Valleys shuddered and jumped to his feet.

Golder stormed past him, followed by the others who were screaming and waving their arms about. Valleys couldn't understand a word of it. He followed Golder as if he were in some kind of nightmare. They were already going down the stairs when a member of the Commission, the only one who hadn't moved, got up and went over to Golder. He had a strange, almost oriental face that was square and flat, and swarthy skin, like dried out earth. He was a former convict. His nose was horribly scarred.

Golder seemed to calm down. The man whispered something in his ear. They went back into the room together and sat down. Simon Alexeevitch began reading again:

'On the annual production of oil estimated at approximately thirty thousand metric tons, the Soviet Government will receive a commission of five per cent. For every ten thousand additional tons, a commission of 0.25 per cent will be added up to an annual yield of four hundred and thirty thousand tons, at which point the Soviet Government will receive a commission of fifteen per cent. The Soviet Treasury will also receive a fee equal to forty-five per cent of the petrol produced from the oil fields and a fee on gas, on a sliding scale from ten per cent to thirty-five per cent, depending on the gasoline it contains . . .'

Golder was resting his hand on his cheek, eyes lowered. listening, without saying a word. Valleys thought he was sleeping: his face, with its deep furrows at the corners of his mouth and pinched nostrils, looked as pale and wan as a corpse.

Valleys looked up at the typed pages of the contract that

Simon Alexeevitch still had in his hands. 'We'll never get through all that in a day . . .' he thought dismally.

Golder suddenly leaned towards him. 'Open that window behind you,' he whispered, 'quickly . . . I'm suffocating . . .'

He made Valleys jump. 'Open it,' ordered Golder again, almost without moving his lips.

Quickly Valleys pushed open the window, then went back to Golder, expecting to find him collapsed in the chair.

Meanwhile, Simon Alexeevitch was still reading:

'The Tübingen Petroleum Company may mine all its crude and refined products without paying a fee and without obtaining special authorisation. In the same way, it may import, duty free, any machinery, tools or primary materials necessary to its operations, along with provisions for its employees . . .'

'Monsieur Golder,' Valleys whispered, 'I'm going to stop him. You're in no condition . . . you're as a white as a ghost . . .'

Golder angrily grabbed his wrist. 'Be quiet! I can't hear what they're saying. Will you be quiet, for God's sake!'

'In exchange for these concessions, the Company must make payments to the Soviet Government, on a sliding scale from five per cent to fifteen per cent of the total yield from the oil fields, and from five per cent to forty per cent of the yield from the active oil wells . . .'

Golder groaned imperceptibly and slumped on to the table. Simon Alexeevitch stopped reading.

'I would like to point out to you that as far as the active oil wells are concerned, the second sub-committee, whose report I have here, has estimated that . . .'

Valleys felt Golder's icy hand grab his own under the table and clutch it anxiously. Automatically, he squeezed Golder's fingers with all his might. He vaguely remembered how he had once held the fractured, bleeding jaw of a dying Irish Setter in the same way. Why did this old Jew so often remind him of a sick dog, close to death, who still bares his teeth, growls wildly and gives one last, powerful bite?

'Your remark regarding Article twenty-seven . . .' said Golder. 'We've hashed that over for three days now; we're not going to start all over again are we? Go on . . .'

'The Tübingen Petroleum Company may construct any buildings, refineries, pipe lines and any other necessary structures. The agreed concessions will remain in force for a period of ninety-nine years . . .'

Golder had pulled his hand away from Valleys' and, with his head on the ink-stained oilcloth, tore open his shirt and began massaging his chest under the table, as if he were trying to expose his lungs to the fresh air. His trembling fingers clutched his heart with the same wild, instinctive desperation of a sick animal who presses the injured part of his body to the ground. He was deathly pale. Valleys watched the sweat pour down his face, thick and heavy, like tears.

But the voice of Simon Alexeevitch had become louder, more solemn. He quietly rose from his chair to conclude:

'Article Seventy-four. Final Article. Once the term of this concession has expired, all the equipment and all the structures on the oil fields heretofore mentioned shall become the sole property of the Soviet Government.'

'It's over,' sighed Valleys, in a kind of trance. Golder pulled himself up and gestured for someone to hand him a pen. The formality of signing the contract began. The ten men were all pale, silent, exhausted.

Eventually, Golder stood up and walked towards the door. The members of the Commission nodded reluctantly to him from their chairs. Only the Chinese representative was smiling. The others looked weary and furious. Golder gave a swift, mechanical nod in reply.

'Now he'll collapse,' thought Valleys. 'He's at death's door . . .'

But he didn't collapse. He walked down the stairs. It wasn't until he was out in the street that he seemed to be gripped by a kind of dizziness. He stopped, pressed his face against a wall, and stood there silently, his whole body shaking.

Valleys called a taxi and helped him into it. Every time they hit a bump in the road, Golder's head swayed and fell forward on to his chest as if he were dead. Gradually, however, the fresh air seemed to revive him. He breathed deeply, putting his hand to his wallet, which lay over his heart.

'Finally, it's over . . . The pigs . . .'

'When I think,' said Valleys, 'that we've been here for four and a half months! When will we be going home, Monsieur Golder? This country is horrible!' he concluded with feeling.

'Yes, it is. You'll leave tomorrow.'

'But what about you?'

'Me . . . I'm going to Teisk.'

'Oh, Monsieur Golder,' said Valleys, upset, 'is that absolutely necessary?'

'Yes. Why?'

Valleys blushed. 'Couldn't I go with you? I really wouldn't like to think you were alone in such a desolate place. You're not well.'

Golder said nothing, then gave a vague, embarrassed shrug. 'You must leave as soon as possible Valleys.'

'But couldn't you . . . get someone else to go with you? It's not safe for you to travel alone in your condition . . .'

'I'm used to it,' Golder muttered sarcastically.

'Room seventeen, first on the left down the corridor,' shouted the porter from below. A moment later, the lights went out. Golder continued climbing the stairs, stumbling on steps that seemed, as in a dream, to go on for ever.

His swollen arm was painful. He put down his suitcase, fumbled around in the dark for the banister, leaned over, called out. But no one replied. He swore in a quiet, breathless voice, climbed up two more steps then stopped, head back, bracing himself against the wall.

The suitcase wasn't really that heavy; all it had inside were his toiletries and a change of clothes. In certain Soviet backwaters there always came a time when you had to carry your own luggage – he'd realised that as soon as he'd left Moscow – but even though his case was very light, he barely had the strength to lift it. He was exhausted.

He had left Teisk the night before. The journey had tired him so much that he'd had to make the driver stop along the way. 'Twenty-two hours in a car!' he groaned, 'Oh, my poor old body!' But he'd been in a broken-down old Ford, and the roads through the mountains were almost impassable. He felt every bump and jolt shoot right through his bones. Towards evening, the car's horn had broken, so the driver had recruited a small boy from the village who climbed on to the running board and, hanging on to the roof with one hand, kept two fingers of the other in his mouth and whistled

142

continuously, from six o'clock until midnight. Even now, Golder could still hear him. He put his hands over his ears and frowned as if in pain. And the rattling the old Ford made, the noise of the windows that seemed about to shatter at every sharp corner . . . It was nearly one o'clock before they finally spotted some lights shimmering in the distance. It was the port, where Golder would go, the next day, to leave for Europe.

In the past, it had been one of the most important trading centres for grain. He knew it well. He'd come here when he was twenty. It was from this port that he had boarded a ship for the very first time.

Now, there were only a few Greek steamers and Soviet cargo ships anchored in the harbour. The town looked so pathetic and abandoned that it was heartbreaking. And his dingy, grubby hotel, with bullet holes in the walls, was inexpressibly sinister. Golder regretted not having left from Moscow as they had suggested at Teisk. These boats hardly ever carried anyone except the 'schouroum-bouroum' – traders from the Levantine who travelled all over the world with their bales of rugs and second-hand fur coats. But one night goes quickly. He was anxious to leave Russia. The following day, he'd be in Constantinople.

He had gone into his room. He let out a deep sigh, switched on the lights and sat down in a corner on the first chair within reach; it was made of a hard, dark wood and with its severe, straight back, it was extremely uncomfortable.

He was so exhausted that the instant he closed his eyes, he lost consciousness and thought he'd fallen asleep. But it had only been a minute. He opened his eyes again and looked absentmindedly around the room. The faint light that shone from the small electric bulb hanging from the ceiling was flickering, as if it would go out at any moment, like a candle in the wind. It lit up some faded paintings: cupids, whose thighs were once rosy, the colour of fresh blood, but were

143

now covered with a thick layer of dust. The high-ceilinged room was vast, with dark furniture covered in red velvet and a table in the middle; on it stood an old oil lamp, whose glass shade was so full of dead flies it looked as if it had been coated in a thick layer of black jam.

There were bullet holes in the walls, of course. On one side in particular, the partition wall was studded with enormous holes; cracks radiated from them like rays of the sun; the plaster was flaking off and crumbling like sand. Golder put his fist into one of the holes, then slowly rubbed his hands together and stood up. It was after three o'clock in the morning.

He took a few steps, then sat back down again to take off his shoes. As he leant forward, he suddenly froze, his arm outstretched. What was the point of getting undressed? He wouldn't be able to sleep. There was no water. He turned one of the taps on the sink. Nothing. It was stifling hot. Not a breath of air. The dust and sweat made his clothes stick to his skin. Whenever he moved, the damp material felt like ice against his shoulders. It sent a little shiver through his body, like a fever.

'Good Lord,' he thought, 'when will I ever get out of this place?'

He felt as if the night would never end. Three more hours to go. The boat was due to leave at dawn. But it would be delayed, naturally . . . Once at sea, he'd feel better. There'd be a bit of wind, a little fresh air. And then Constantinople. The Mediterranean. Paris. Paris? He felt a vague satisfaction at the thought of all those bastards at the Stock Exchange. He could just hear them: 'Have you heard about Golder? . . . Well, who'd have believed it? . . . He really looked like he was finished . . .' Filthy bastards. What would the Teisk shares be worth now? He tried to work it out, but it was too difficult. Since Valleys had left, he'd had no news from Europe. All in good time . . . He let out a deep sigh. It was strange, he couldn't imagine what his life would be like when the journey was over. All in good time . . . Joy . . . He frowned slightly. Joy . . . Every now and then she would remember her old dad's existence, but only when she or her husband had lost money gambling, of course. Then she would come to see him, take some more money and disappear again for months on end . . . He had expressly instructed Seton that she was not allowed to touch her capital. 'Otherwise, from the day she gets married to the day I die . . .' He stopped himself. He had no illusions. 'I've done everything I can,' he said out loud, sadly.

He had taken off his shoes. He went and stretched out on the bed. But for some time now, he had been unable to lie down for long. He couldn't breathe. Sometimes he would fall asleep, but then he would immediately start suffocating and wake up to the distant sound of crying – strange, pitiful cries that came as if from some dream, and which seemed to him terrifying, incomprehensible and threatening. He didn't realise that it was he who was crying out; the childlike sobs were his own.

Now, once more, as soon as he had lain down, he began to suffocate. With great difficulty, he pulled himself from the bed, dragged a chair over to the window and opened it. Below was the port, dark water . . . Day was breaking.

Suddenly, he fell asleep.

At five o'clock, the first blasts of the port sirens woke Golder.

He had difficulty picking up his shoes and there was still no water when he tried the tap on the sink. He rang for the porter and waited a long time, but nobody came. Eventually, he found a little Eau de Cologne in a bottle in his suitcase and rubbed it on his hands and face. Then he got his things together and went downstairs.

It was only once he was downstairs that he managed to get a cup of tea. He paid, then left.

Through habit, he started looking around for a taxi. But the town seemed deserted. A cloud of sand, carried inland by the sea breeze, obscured all the buildings. It lay so thick on the streets that there were deep footprints where people had walked past, as if through snow. Golder motioned to a young boy who was silently running barefoot along the middle of the street.

'Can you carry my suitcase to the port? Aren't there any taxis?'

The child seemed not to understand. But he took hold of the suitcase and walked on ahead.

The houses were all closed, their windows boarded up. There were banks, official buildings, but empty, deserted. On the walls, the outline of the Imperial Eagle remained etched into the stone, like a wound . . . Instinctively, Golder walked more quickly.

146

He vaguely recognised certain old, dark alleyways, the houses made of rickety wood. But it was so silent . . . Suddenly, he stopped.

They weren't far from the port. The air had the strong smell of mud and salt. A small, dark shoemaker's shop, with its iron boot swinging in front of the window, creaking . . . On the corner opposite, his old lodging house, a place frequented by sailors and prostitutes . . . The shoemaker was one of his father's cousins who had settled in the town; Golder used to go and have a meal with him from time to time. He remembered the place well . . . He made an effort to try to recall what his cousin looked like. But all he could remember was the sound of his bitter, plaintive voice, probably because it was just like Soifer's: 'Stay here, my boy . . . Do you think you're going to find gold on the streets somewhere else? Ha! Life is hard wherever you go.'

Without thinking, Golder started to turn the door handle, then let his hand drop back down to his side. It had been forty-eight years! He shrugged his shoulders, kept walking.

'I wonder what would have happened if I'd stayed?' He laughed bitterly. 'Who knows? Imagine Gloria doing the housework and frying potato pancakes in goose fat on Friday night. Life . . .' he whispered softly. How odd it was that after so many years, he should be brought back to this desolate place . . .

The port. He recognised it as clearly as if he had left the day before. The little Customs building, half in ruins. Beached boats buried in the black sand, which was littered with bits of coal and rubbish; watermelon rind and dead animals bobbing in the deep, muddy green water, just as in the past.

He climbed on board a small Greek steamship that used to do the crossing between Batoum and Constantinople, before the war. It must have been a passenger boat, for it seemed to have certain amenities. There was a sitting room, a piano. But since the Revolution, it had carried only merchandise – and strange merchandise at that. It was dirty and run down.

'Thank goodness the crossing won't take long . . .' thought Golder.

On the bridge, a few *schouroum-bouroum* in their red skullcaps were sitting on the floor, playing cards. They looked up when Golder walked by. One of them waved a pink glass necklace that was hanging from his arm and smiled: 'Buy something, good sir . . .' Golder shook his head and gently pushed them aside with his cane. How many times, during his first crossing – a crossing whose memory clung to him with a strange, tenacious persistence – had he played cards with men just like these, at night, in some corner of the boat . . . That was so long ago . . . They moved back to let him pass. He went down into his cabin and looked with a sigh at the sea through the porthole. The boat was moving. He sat down on his berth, a plank of wood covered with a thin, prickly straw mattress. If the weather held, he would sleep on the bridge. But the wind was blowing fiercely and the boat was being tossed about. Golder looked at the sea with a kind of hatred. He was so weary of this endlessly changing world – the landscape rushing past train and car windows, these waves that roared like animals, the trails of smoke in the stormy autumn sky. If only the horizon could be still until he died . . . 'I'm tired,' he murmured. With that instinctive, nervous gesture of people with a heart condition, he pressed both hands against his chest. He massaged it gently as if it were a child or a dying animal – to encourage the worn-out, stubborn machine that beat so feebly in his old body.

Suddenly, after a particularly strong roll of the ship, he seemed to feel his heart falter, then start beating faster, too fast . . . At the same time, he was struck by an excruciating pain in his left shoulder. He went pale, sat with his head hanging forward, looking terrified, and waited for a long time. The sound of his breathing seemed to fill the cabin, drowning out the noise of the wind and the sea.

Little by little, the pain eased off, then stopped completely. 'It was nothing,' he said out loud, forcing himself to smile. 'It's over.'

He was having difficulty breathing. 'Over . . .' he sighed more quietly.

He tried to stand. Outside, the sky and the sea had grown gradually darker. The cabin was as black as if it were the middle of the night. The only light came from the porthole, a strange green murky glow that was not really light at all. Golder fumbled about for his coat, put it on, then went out. He stretched out his hands in front of him, like a blind man. Each time the sea struck the boat, it shuddered, reeled and plunged, as if it were about to disappear, dragged down into the water. He grasped the bottom of the little ladder that led to the bridge, and hauled himself up.

'Be careful, Comrade, there's a strong wind up there!' shouted one of the sailors who came running. Golder could smell the strong odour of alcohol on his breath.

'We're being tossed about, Comrade . . .'

'I'm used to it,' Golder grumbled sarcastically.

But he had difficulty making it to the bridge. Great swells of water were crashing against the boat. In one corner, the *schouroum-bouroum* were huddled in a heap underneath a soaking wet tarpaulin, shivering like a mournful herd of frozen cattle. One of them saw Golder, looked up and shouted a few words in a shrill, plaintive voice that was drowned out in the commotion. Golder gestured that he couldn't hear him. The man repeated what he'd said louder, tensing up his pale face and rolling his blazing eyes. Then suddenly he succumbed to a bout of seasickness, and fell back on to the deck; he lay motionless on his old sheepskin, amongst the bales of cargo and other men.

Golder walked past them.

149

Soon he had to stop. He stood still, bent over, like a tree yielding to a violent wind; his face was strained and on his lips was the sharp, bitter taste of salt and the sea. He tried to open his eyes but couldn't; he was clutching a wet, icy-cold iron railing that was freezing his fingers.

As each wave crashed into the boat, it seemed to sink further, breaking under the weight of the sea; every now and then, a long, hollow, heart-rending groan rose up from its timbers, drowning out the harsh sound of the wind and the waves.

'Well,' thought Golder, 'this was all I needed . . .'

Nevertheless, he didn't move. With an odd sort of pleasure, he let the storm batter his old body. The sea water, mingling with the rain, soaked his cheeks, his lips; his eyelashes and hair were caked with salt.

Suddenly, he heard a voice shouting loudly, very close to him, but the wind drowned out the words. Struggling to look up, he vaguely made out the shape of a man, doubled over, hanging on to the rail with both hands.

A wave crashed into Golder, breaking at his feet. He could feel the water filling his eyes and mouth. He quickly jumped back. The other man followed him. With the storm knocking them against the wall with each step, they managed to stagger below deck.

'What horrible weather . . .' the man murmured in Russian, sounding terrified, 'Dear God, what horrible weather . . .'

It was pitch black, and all Golder could see was a kind of long overcoat dragging along the floor, but he recognised the lilting accent all too well.

'Is this your first crossing?' he asked. 'You're a Yid?'

The man laughed nervously but seemed cheered. 'Yes,' he murmured. 'You too?'

'Me too,' said Golder.

Golder had sat down on the old, tattered velvet settee fixed to the wall. The man remained standing in front of

150

him. With numb hands, Golder fumbled in his jacket pocket
for his cigarette case, opened it and held it out. 'Have one.'

When he lit the match, he looked up for a moment and
studied the face of the man bending towards him; he was
young, barely more than a teenager, pale, with a long, sad
nose, curly black woolly hair and enormous, anxious eyes.

'Where are you from?'

'Kremenetz, Sir, in the Ukraine.'

'I've been there,' murmured Golder.

In the past, it had been a miserable village where black
pigs had rolled about in the mud with Jewish children. It
probably hadn't changed much.

'So, you're leaving? For good?'

'Oh, yes.'

'Why are you leaving now? I know why we left in my
day!'

'Ah, Sir,' said the little Jew with an accent that was comical
and tragic both at the same time, 'do things ever change for
people like us? I'm an honest young man, I am, Sir, and yet I
just got out of prison two days ago. And why? Because an
order came through to take some boxes of 'Montpensiers' –
you know, those candied fruits? – from the south to Moscow.
It was summer and stifling hot; of course everything melted in
the freight cars. When I got to Moscow they were dripping
through the crates. But was that my fault? I spent eighteen
months in prison for that. I'm free now. I want to go to Europe.'

'How old are you?'

'Eighteen, Sir.'

'Ah . . .' said Golder slowly. 'About the same age as me,
when I left.'

'Are you from here?'

'Yes.'

The young man fell silent. He smoked with obvious
pleasure. In the darkness, Golder could see his hands, lit up
by the cigarette; they were shaking.

'Your first crossing . . .' Golder said again. 'So where are you going?'

'Paris, to start with. I have a cousin who's a tailor in Paris. He moved there before the war. But as soon as I have enough money, I'm going to New York! Yes, New York!' he repeated excitedly.

But Golder wasn't listening. Instead, he observed, with a kind of sad, poignant pleasure, the way the boy in front of him moved his hands and shoulders; the way his whole body trembled incessantly as he tripped over his words in his eagerness to speak. That feverish desire, that nervous energy . . . he, too, had once possessed them: the hungry exuberance so particular to young people of his race. All that was so long ago now . . .

'You know you're going to starve to death, don't you?' he said sharply.

'Oh, I'm used to that . . .'

'Yes . . . But over there, it's harder . . .'

'What's the difference? It won't be for long . . .'

Golder suddenly burst out laughing, a laugh as dry and sharp as a whip.

'So that's what you think, do you? Well, you're a fool! It lasts for years, years . . . And after that, to tell the truth, it's hardly any better . . .'

'After that . . .' the boy whispered passionately, 'after that you get rich . . .'

'After that,' replied Golder, 'you die, alone, like a dog, the same way you lived . . .'

He stopped talking and threw back his head with a stifled moan. Once again he felt that excruciating pain around his shoulder, and his aching heart seemed to stop beating . . .

'You don't look well . . .' he heard the boy say. 'Is it seasickness?'

'No,' said Golder, his voice weak and stuttering. 'No . . . it's my heart . . .'

152

He was having trouble breathing; it hurt him to speak. But what did the past, *his* past, matter to this little fool anyway? Life was different now . . . easier. Besides, he didn't really give a damn about this little Jew, for God's sake . . .

'For someone who's been through as much as I have, my boy, seasickness and foolish things like that . . . So, you want to get rich?'

He lowered his voice.

'Take a good look at me. Do you think it's worth it?'

He'd let his head fall forwards on to his chest. For a moment, he felt as if the noise of the wind and the sea were fading away into the distance, merging into a kind of chant . . . Then, suddenly, he heard the terrified voice of the boy shouting 'Help!' He stood up, staggered forward, stretched both arms up, clutching at the air, the void. Then he collapsed on to the floor.

Some time later he came round, as if dragged out of deep, dark water. He was semi-conscious, stretched out on his cabin bed. Someone had opened his shirt and slipped a rolled-up overcoat underneath his head. At first, he thought he was alone. Then, when he began feverishly to look around the room, he heard the voice of the little Jew behind him.

'Sir . . .' he whispered.

Golder tried to raise his hand. The boy leaned towards him. 'Oh, Sir! Are you feeling better?'

Golder moved his lips as if he had forgotten the shape and sound of human speech. Finally, he managed to murmur, 'Light.'

The light was switched on and he sighed in pain. He moved, and gave a moan. Instinctively he reached for his chest, to touch his heart, but his heavy hands fell back down to his sides. He muttered a few confused words in a foreign language, and then seemed to come round completely. He opened his eyes. 'Go and get the captain,' he said, his voice strangely clear.

The boy went out. Golder was alone. He groaned slightly when a particularly strong wave hit the boat. But the rolling gradually subsided. Sunlight shone in through the porthole. Golder, exhausted, closed his eyes.

When the Greek captain, a large drunken man, came in, Golder appeared to be asleep.

154

'What's going on? Is he dead?' the captain asked, swearing.

Golder slowly turned his head towards the captain's hollow, pale face, with its pinched, white lips.

'Stop the boat . . .' he whispered.

When the captain didn't reply, he said it again, louder: 'Stop. Do you understand?'

Golder's eyes, half-hidden beneath his quivering eyelids, burned so fiercely that the captain was confused; he shrugged his shoulders: 'You're crazy.'

'I'll pay you . . . I'll give you a thousand pounds.'

'Mad,' the captain growled. 'He's on his way out . . . I'd bet my own life on it . . . What did I do to deserve a passenger like this?'

'Back to shore . . .' Golder mumbled, then, 'Do you want me to die here all alone, like an animal? Bastard . . .' And then something no one could make out.

'Isn't there a doctor on board?' the boy asked. But the captain had already left.

The young lad went over to Golder who was panting desperately.

'Try to be patient,' he whispered softly, 'we'll soon be in Constantinople . . . We're moving quickly now . . . The storm has stopped. Do you know anyone in Constantinople? Do you have any relatives there? Anyone at all?'

'What?' murmured Golder. 'What was that?'

He finally seemed to understand, but all he kept saying was 'What?' over and over again. Then he fell silent.

The boy continued whispering anxiously: 'Constantinople . . . It's a big city . . . they can look after you there . . . you'll soon get well . . . Don't be afraid.'

But at that moment, he realised that Golder was dying. For the first time, the hollow sound of death rose from his tortured chest.

It went on for nearly an hour. The boy was shivering. Even so, he didn't leave. He listened to the air reverberating in the dying man's throat with a deep, husky groan, like some mysterious force, as if an alien being had already taken over his body.

'It won't be long now,' he thought, 'then it will all be over. I'll leave him then . . . I don't even know his name, for God's sake!'

Then he looked over at the wallet stuffed full of English money that had fallen to the floor when he had carried him over to the bed. He bent down, picked it up, looked inside, then sighed, and holding his breath, slipped it gently into Golder's open hand – a swollen, heavy, icy hand, the hand of a corpse.

'Who knows? That way . . . Maybe he'll come round for a moment before he dies. He might want to give me some money . . . Who knows? Who can know? I'm the one who's stayed with him. He's all alone.'

He began to wait. The sea grew calmer as night fell. The boat glided calmly along. The wind had dropped. 'It will be a beautiful night,' the boy thought.

He stretched out his hand to touch the wrist dangling in front of him; the pulse was beating so faintly that the sound of the watch, with its leather strap, almost drowned it out. Golder was still alive, though. The body is reluctant to die. He was alive. He opened his eyes. He said something. But the air was still growling in his chest with a sinister, chilling sound, like floodwaters receding. The boy leant over him, listening intently. Golder said a few words in Russian, then suddenly the forgotten language of his childhood unexpectedly spilled from his lips and he started speaking Yiddish.

He spoke quickly, in a strange, mumbling voice that was interrupted now and again by long, hoarse wheezing. Sometimes he would stop, slowly bringing his hands to his throat, as if to lift some invisible weight. Half of his face was paralysed, one eye already clouded over and staring. But the other eye was alive, piercing. Sweat poured down his cheeks. The boy wanted to wipe it away. 'Never mind . . .' Golder groaned, 'There's no point . . . Listen. In Paris, you must go to Maître Seton, Rue Albert, number twenty-eight. You must tell him that Golder is dead. Say it. Say it again. Seton, Maître Seton, lawyer. Give him everything in my suitcase and wallet. Tell him I want him to do whatever he thinks best . . . for my daughter . . . Then you must go to see Tübingen . . . Wait.'

He was panting. His lips were moving, but the boy couldn't understand what he was saying. He leaned so far over him that he could smell the dying man's breath, the fever coming from Golder's mouth.

'Hotel Continental. Write it down,' Golder finally whispered. 'John Tübingen. Hotel Continental.'

The boy hurriedly took an old letter from his pocket, tore off the back of the envelope and wrote down the two addresses.

'You will tell him that Golder is dead,' he ordered, his voice fading, 'that I beg him to look after my daughter's interests . . . that I trust him and . . .'

He stopped. His eyes were darting about, their light edging towards darkness.

'And . . . No. Just that. That's all. Yes, that's fine.'

He looked at the bit of paper that the young boy was holding in his hand.

'Give it to me . . . I'll sign it . . . That would be best . . .'

'I don't think you'll manage it,' said the boy. Nevertheless, he took Golder's hand and slipped the pencil between his weak fingers.

'I don't think you'll manage it,' he said again.

'Golder . . .' the dying man whispered, 'David Golder . . .' with a kind of madness and terrified determination – the name, the syllables that formed it, sounding as incomprehensible to him as the words of some unknown language . . . Nevertheless, he managed to sign.

'I'll give you all the money I have with me,' he whispered, 'but you must swear to do everything exactly as I've said.'

'Yes, I swear it.'

'Before Almighty God,' said Golder.

'Before Almighty God.'

A sudden convulsion ran through his face, and blood started pouring from the corners of his mouth on to his hands. His rattled breathing eased.

'Sir, can you still hear me?' the boy asked, fearfully.

The evening light pouring in from the porthole fell straight on to Golder's face. The boy shuddered. This time it really was the end. The wallet remained open in the outstretched hand. He grabbed it, counted the money, slipped it into his pocket, then put the envelope with the two addresses under his belt.

'Is he finally dead?' he thought.

He reached out towards Golder's open shirt, but his hands were shaking so violently that he couldn't manage to feel whether the heart was still beating.

He left him there. He walked backwards towards the door on tiptoe, as if he were afraid to waken him. Then, without looking back, he ran out.

Golder was alone.

He had the still, frozen look of a corpse. But death had not claimed him suddenly, all at once, like a wave. He had felt himself losing his voice, the heat of life, losing consciousness of the man he had once been. But right until the end, he could see. He watched as the light of the setting sun spilled over the sea, saw how the water sparkled.

And, deep from within his memory, until he drew his final breath, certain images continued to flash before him, fainter and more indistinct as death drew nearer. For a moment, he thought he was actually touching Joyce's hair, her skin. Then she seemed to pull away, to abandon him, as he plunged deeper into darkness. One last time, he thought he could hear her laugh, light and sweet, like a bell ringing in the distance. Then she was gone. He saw Marcus. Certain faces, vague shapes, as if carried along by the water at dusk, would swirl around for a moment, then disappear. And, as he reached the end, all he could see was a shop, lit up, on a dark street, a street from his childhood, a candle set behind an icy window, the night, snow falling, and himself . . . He could feel snowflakes on his lips, which melted with the taste of ice and water so familiar to him from the past. And he could hear someone calling: 'David, David . . .' A voice hushed by the snow, the low, dark sky . . . A small voice that suddenly grew fainter and faded away, as if disappearing in a different direction. It was the last sound he was to hear on this earth.

BY IRÈNE NÉMIROVSKY
ALSO AVAILABLE FROM VINTAGE

| Suite Française | 9780099488781 | £7.99 |

FREE POST AND PACKING
Overseas customers allow £2.00 per paperback

BY PHONE: 01624 677237

BY POST: Random House Books
C/o Bookpost, PO Box 29, Douglas
Isle of Man, IM99 1BQ

BY FAX: 01624 670923

BY EMAIL: bookshop@enterprise.net

Cheques (payable to Bookpost) and credit cards accepted

Prices and availability subject to change without notice.
Allow 28 days for delivery.
When placing your order, please mention if you do not wish to receive
any additional information

www.randomhouse.co.uk/vintage